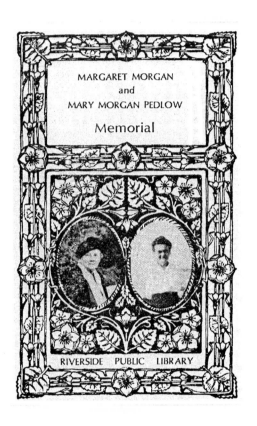

MARGARET MORGAN
and
MARY MORGAN PEDLOW

Memorial

RIVERSIDE PUBLIC LIBRARY

Matchit

Also by Martha Moore

UNDER THE MERMAID ANGEL

ANGELS ON THE ROOF

Matchit

Martha Moore

DELACORTE PRESS

Published by
Delacorte Press
an imprint of
Random House Children's Books
a division of Random House, Inc.
1540 Broadway
New York, New York 10036

Visit us on the Web! www.randomhouse.com/kids
Educators and librarians, for a variety of teaching tools, visit us at
www.randomhouse.com/teachers

Library of Congress Cataloging-in-Publication Data

Moore, Martha (Martha A.)
    Matchit / Martha Moore.
        p. cm.
    Summary: After his father leaves him with an old acquaintance in Texas, a
resentful twelve-year-old boy lives by an auto junkyard while waiting for his
father's return.
    ISBN 0-385-90023-6 (lib. bdg.) — ISBN 0-385-72906-5
    [1. Fathers and sons—Fiction. 2. Automobile graveyards—Fiction.
3. Self-esteem—Fiction. 4. Emotional problems—Fiction. 5. Texas—
Fiction.] I. Title.
    PZ7.M78715 Mat 2002
    [Fic]—dc21

2001032469

The text of this book is set in 11-point New Century Schoolbook.

Book design by Saho Fujii

Manufactured in the United States of America

April 2002

10   9   8   7   6   5   4   3   2   1

BVG

To every one of us who loses hope
and every one of us who helps another find it

Acknowledgments

Thank you to . . .

Hannah Goolsby, who always sees the best in every child
Amanda Jenkins, who always saw the best in Matchit

Karen Wojtyla for being so gifted and talented

LB Jackson for telling me how it is

Howard for loving pigeons and fish

Peter and Michael for listening

And all the boys at school who make great car sounds
and love to talk about wheels

Prologue

I HELD THE BIRD AND ZEBBY SEWED.

There was a zig-zaggy rip like a great big jack-o'-lantern grin on his neck, but Zebby sewed quick like he'd done it a million times. The whole time he was grumbling. He'd sewed up plenty of stuff, even his own leg, but he never thought he'd be sewing up a pigeon throat.

My brain said Why are you doing it? This bird's wings quit twitching the first time the needle poked through. His eyes look like somebody turned out the lights. No way this bird is going to make it.

Then I felt something. It was his heart. It was beating bumpity against the inside of my fingers. I wanted to holler. I wanted to jump up, but I didn't dare. One sound, one move, might have scared him into dying.

When Zebby was finished, he walked off. He didn't smile, frown, nothing. That man's got a face that's rusted in place. I figure it's because he's lived in a junkyard too long. It's a joke, but it's the truth, too. That's where we both live, smack-dab in the middle of Babe's Body Parts where the red-and-white sign says We Take In Your Wrecked Cars and Other Junk.

That bird that got sewed, I named him. Dog. Wouldn't nothing mess with him now.

My brain said Matchit, you slow boy. Naming a half-dead bird. You dumb or what? Everything you touch messes up. Don't you know this old bird will wind up in the trash bin? Don't you know you're the bad-luck boy?

It's true. There was only one time I was lucky. That was a long time before I came to the junkyard. It was when I got to go to the mountains and fish in a trout stream. Up there the water is so clean and cold, and so pretty. You can pinch you a little yellow salmon egg out of the jar and push it on a hook and after you throw in the line, you can see it shining down in the water. You know pretty soon a fish will come along and snap it up. The feeling is real exciting, like I don't know what.

Daddy always says, Match, you can't remember that camping trip. You weren't even big enough to hold a fishing pole.

My daddy, he don't know nothing.

At night, I lie in my bed on the screened-in porch and look out over the junkyard. When the moon is full, it lights up the whole place, making weird kinds of shapes everywhere, and you can hear the thump thump thump of cat paws jumping on the car roofs. Babe's pigeons are cooing that underwater gurgling sound they make, and I pretend the moon is hanging by a piece of fishing line.

All of us, the stray cats, Babe and me, Zebby, even the pigeons, are the fish swimming around that huge bobber moon like we think it's something safe. You never know, though, when it'll jerk up all the sudden and pull one of us up, screaming and kicking into a place where we can't breathe.

I can work myself up into some kind of predicament, feeling all sweaty and cold at the same time, glad I have a place to sleep on the back porch, but scared, too, like the cars are lying dead at the bottom of the lake and I'm swimming around them trying to hide.

Finally, about the time I get my eyes closed, I get waked up.

Sparks are flying way over around Zebby's place out on the edge of the yard. The hot of the day has finally worn off, and he's at work, welding crashed-up car parts. I lie in bed watching those sparks fly into the dark, falling like little stars on Zebby's arms, and then I start thinking again.

What if we're not fish and the moon's not a fishing bobber and we're all part of this gigantic sculpture that someone else is building out of all the scraps of the world?

My brain says Which do you want, Matchit? Swimming and hiding or being stuck like a welded piece of scrap metal?

Neither one sounds good to me. I turn my head to the wall and go to sleep. I don't dream about nothing.

Chapter ONE

IT IS EIGHT O'CLOCK IN THE MORNING.

I'm standing at the bathroom door, hoping and trying to change my daddy's mind. He leans across the sink in his new black Wranglers. His brand-new Garth Brooks shirt sits on the toilet seat, still folded in the package.

I've been thinking about what to say, and now it's time. I take a deep breath, and my words march out of my mouth like they think they're the Pledge of Allegiance.

"If you let me go with you, I promise to mind you. I promise I won't complain. I'll do whatever you say. And I'll be nice to Jewel. I promise."

He don't say nothing.

Jewel is my daddy's girlfriend. She's what made him lose every crumb of sense he ever had.

I watch him squeeze a blob of gel on his palm, rub his hands together, then wipe it through his hair, making the black even shinier. He combs it straight back. It's like somebody on TV, but I forget who.

"I won't talk back, neither."

Still, nothing.

"If we have a flat, I'll change it. I'll check the oil and change it, too. I'm the one who knew we needed an alternator. Remember when the truck wouldn't start smooth and it was making that zrrrrr . . . zrrr . . . zrrrrrr sound every time you turned the ignition? I said I bet it's the alternator, and Jake thought it was the starter. Remember, I was right?"

He sets his comb down on the edge of the sink and talks to my reflection in the mirror.

"Match, you can't go and that's that." He turns on the faucet and washes his hands and dries them on a towel. "You'll just have to stay at Babe's a couple of days. When Jake gets back, you can go to his place."

"I'll run away you make me stay with Jake. I mean it."

Jake is Daddy's first cousin, which makes him my second, but I don't claim him as any kind of kin. I call him Jake the Jerk. He stomps around in his alligator boots trying to make the ground think he's important. Jake is grown, but he thinks it's fun to tease kids, scare them, too.

He's got this fish-boning knife. It's so sharp it can cut a hair in half. One night real late when I had to stay with him, he snuck into the kitchen where I sleep at his place. I was on my cot inside my sleeping bag, not thinking about nothing. All the sudden, he zipped me up, head and all.

Then he poked me with that knife. Scared the pee out of me. Jake, he loves jokes as long as they're not on him.

"I want to go with you," I beg Daddy.

"Don't be stubborn, Matchit," Daddy says. He's holding his razor at the edge of one of his sideburns again, trying to make a perfect straight line across the bottom.

"School's out, I won't be getting into no fights. I won't get in trouble. Please, Daddy."

"It's not the fights. You know why you can't go." He puts his face up close to the mirror. "These look even to you, Match?"

I don't answer that question, and he gives me a look that says Jewel comes first. That I'll always be around, but she might not be.

The way I figure it is I had dibs on him before she did. I know he won't listen, though.

He says, "Look, your birthday's coming up. I'll be back way before then. If for some reason I'm not back, I'll send for you. Tell you what, you can ride on an airplane. First class. I'll tell them to bring you all the peanuts and Cokes you want, pizza, too, if you want. Maybe I could talk to the captain, see if you could go in the cockpit and watch him fly the plane. How would you like that?"

My daddy adds on promises like somebody laying bricks without any cement. He keeps on going like he don't know when to stop.

"I'll get you that bike you wanted," he says. "One of those color electronic pocket games, too, if you want. You know I wouldn't miss your birthday for a million dollars."

He picks up his shirt from the top of the toilet seat, takes it out of the package, unfolds it, and slides his arms in real careful like he's afraid to touch anything. He unzips his pants and tucks the shirttail in smooth all the way around on top of his underwear. He wants to look good for Jewel.

"Start getting ready," he tells me.

I have to look good, too, not for Jewel, but for Babe, a woman I don't even know, a woman my daddy is hoping like crazy will want me to stay.

First I have to take a bath with Lifebuoy deodorant soap and splash Old Spice on my neck. I have to clip my fingernails and put on new underwear, new jeans, a new button shirt, and never-been-worn socks. When I get finished, I feel too new and too stiff. I feel like I'm wrapped in a Band-Aid.

Daddy slaps water on top of my hair and parts it on the side. He steps back and gives me the once-over.

"You're looking good, boy."

I don't say nothing.

My heart is squeezing up tight against my new shirt. It's making a whole lot of noise.

The only thing is, nobody can hear it but me.

Chapter TWO

WE'RE ON HIGHWAY 287 HEADING NORTH. Daddy's got his foot pressed to the gas, as far as it can go, nearly. He's staring straight ahead out the windshield. His mind is a million miles away. All he can think about is Jewel. She's probably all fixed up in a church dress and high heels, waiting on him to hurry up and dump me and come get her.

Pretty soon they will be on their way to Mount Rushmore. That's where those dead presidents got their faces carved in the side of a mountain. Jewel's biggest dream in the whole wide world is to climb to the top and stand in George Washington's eyelid. She begged Daddy to take her. And it had to be quick or never.

There was only one problem. She didn't want to take me.

I'm sitting here in the truck beside him. My hands are sweaty and my heart is beating too fast. My brain is dogging me like crazy. It's asking me so many questions I feel like punching somebody. What if Babe don't want you to stay? Then what? What if she does want you? Then what? What's it like sleeping in a pile of junk? And the worst question: What if Daddy gets so wrapped up in Jewel, he don't come back at all?

I know junkyards got rats. They got snakes, too. When I was a little kid, we went looking for parts at Best Buy Auto Salvage, which is bigger and closer than Babe's. We'd get to the yard, and Daddy would say, "Hold my hand, Match, and don't let go. A rat living under one of these old cars could eat you up in one gulp." He'd take his time, too, knocking on every hood trying to see if there was an engine inside, kicking on every tire. The whole time I'd squeeze his hand like crazy, scared to death. You never know when a rattlesnake or copperhead might jump out from underneath a car frame and get you good.

I don't like junkyards.

Just thinking about sleeping in one makes my stomach get tight. It feels like a rubber band that's stretched, ready to shoot. I reach down to loosen my belt. I forgot. I don't even got a belt.

My brain says You really done it this time, bad-luck boy. You messed up good. How many chances did you get to do right? Plenty. At school they gave you about ten new chances every day, but did you change yourself around? No, you didn't. You are getting just what you deserve. Maybe if you live in a junkyard for a while, you'll learn to be sorrier for who you are. And something else, Buster . . . if you get scared, nobody's going to hold your hand.

So what. I don't want nobody holding my hand. I'll fight anybody who tries to.

"Is the transmission slipping again?" I ask.

Daddy says, "Nope."

"Do you really think this old truck can make it all the way to South Dakota?"

"Yep."

"Did you check all the belts?"

"Yep."

"How about the timing chain? We got over two hundred thousand miles. That chain goes out, you're sunk. If it ruins the valves, you're looking at a whole lot of money."

"I'm going, Matchit," he says, staring straight ahead at the yellow lines on the highway. "I have to. I'll never know if this can work if I don't."

With Jewel, it won't work. I guarantee it. But you can't tell him. My daddy's brain is stuck in one gear. I know how stubborn he is. I've lived with him for almost twelve years, most of my life, just me and him. You want to know what happened to my mama? She messed up too much. That's all I got to say about her right now.

"I don't want to stay with this Babe lady. She don't even know I'm coming." He squeezes the steering wheel with both hands and stares straight ahead. I look out the side window. We're passing a whole lot of nothing. Just trash blowed up against fences.

11

"I hate junkyards."

Daddy whistles air through his teeth. He hits the gas harder.

"This woman don't even know me." I got to make sure he knows that. "I don't think it's a good idea to leave a kid with a stranger. You ever heard of stranger danger?"

"I know her real well, Match. I told you that. We worked together a few months."

"How do you know she'd want to keep a kid? Some people hate kids."

"Not Babe. She loves kids. She's a real nice lady. Besides, she owes me a favor. One thing about Babe Clark, she always pays up."

I know the story. She really needed work, and Daddy helped her line up some jobs trimming houses.

"You could've called her first."

He won't answer that one, but I know why he didn't call. My daddy is proud with a capital *P*. He don't ask nobody for nothing, not unless it's Jake. With Babe, he's counting on we can show up and hint around, and she'll offer to let me stay.

"What if nobody's home?"

"She's there. I called and got directions."

"She recognize your voice?"

"Nope."

"I thought you were good friends."

He sighs again, long and hard. "It's been a while since she heard my voice. That don't mean nothing."

He's got on his dark aviator sunglasses that cost twenty-nine dollars. They hide his eyes real good. I wonder if Babe will even remember who he is. It's been ten years, at least.

"Her place should be coming up pretty soon." Daddy eases up on the gas. "First there's supposed to be a convenience store called Lucky's. After that comes a taxidermy shop, then we go about a half mile, and we're supposed to see a red-and-white sign advertising the junkyard. Another quarter of a mile and we should be there."

I got one fingernail I've been chewing on. It's bit down too far, and when I can taste the blood in my mouth, I pull it out and wipe my mouth with the back of my hand. I got a stripe of blood smeared across my thumb.

"Matchit!" Daddy takes his foot off the gas and steps on the brake. He shifts into second, and the truck veers to the shoulder. Finally, we slow to a stop.

"What are you doing?" he says. "Let me see that finger."

I hold it out and he examines it. Shakes his head. "Come on, Match," he says. "It's not that bad. Be tough."

We're right in front of a funny-looking blue house with about a hundred dead animals looking out the front window. There's squirrels, snakes, raccoons, chickens, you name it. The sign says Sister's Taxidermy, which means we are almost to the junkyard. It seems to me like those animals are trying to tell us something. Don't go one step farther. Not one inch. Don't go to the junkyard. You'll be sorry.

Daddy pulls his clean handkerchief out of his pocket and unfolds it. He hands it to me. The blood soaks through the white in a red streak.

"I want to go with you," I tell him.

He takes a long breath and lets it out slow. "When I get back in a few days," he says, "maybe we can drive down to Lake Fork. We'll rent us a fishing boat. Maybe we'll even hire a guide to help us find the big fish. We'll be sure to catch something. Maybe you can hook you a nine-pound bass. Then we can drive down here to the taxidermist and get it mounted. We'll get a little brass name tag on it saying Caught by Matchit McCarty. How about that?"

He's trying to make himself feel better about leaving me. I know what it is. It's called a guilt trip. That's what Jewel said he keeps going on. I heard her talking to him one night when they thought I was asleep. She said a man ought to think about himself, about his girlfriend.

"You okay?" Daddy asks. "Stop biting on your fingernails."

He starts the truck and we're on our way again. My stomach feels tight. Every second it squeezes up tighter and tighter. It's like a balloon you've blown up too much and you know any minute it will pop. Every time I throw up, my stomach feels this way. To tell you the truth, I hope I do throw up. That would cause a big problem. Nobody wants to keep a kid with urp all over him. I know Babe wouldn't. Urp is bad if it's your own kid, but it's especially bad if you don't know the kid. Daddy would end up having to take me with him, and Jewel would refuse to climb into the truck because it would smell so bad, even if we did clean it all up. Daddy would have to give up this crazy idea, and we could go home.

Everything could get back to exactly the way it used to be.

We travel down the road a few yards, and I decide that the first time he turns his head to look out, I will jab my finger down my throat. I can do it. I've done it plenty of times to get out of going to school.

You poke your middle finger as far as it will go into your throat, all the way to the back. You gag a couple of times. Then you urp. It's easy.

"What the . . . ," Daddy hollers when he hears me choking. He veers to the shoulder again and slams on the brake. "Don't you dare!" He's in a panic.

"Get out of the truck." I slide out and walk a few steps into the weeds at the side of the road.

"You see what time it's getting to be?" he says, tapping his watch. It's already ten. Now he's really getting worried. Not about me. About Jewel. She don't like him being late. If this plan falls through and Babe don't keep me, he's cooked. No way Jewel wants me tagging along.

"Please, Matchit. I need your help."

He looks like he's about to cry. He's not going to be in any kind of good mood for Jewel. That I'm glad about.

Pretty soon after we've headed back down the road again, we see Babe's big red-and-white sign, and a little farther, we see the junkyard. It don't look like nothing, just part double-wide trailer, part house, built on. Somebody

15

took the wheels off the trailer and nailed the whole thing to the ground. It ain't going nowhere. All around it, as far as I can see, falling over the edge of the world almost, is a big pile of junk, a garbage dump of wrecked cars and trucks.

My brain says Ha! Welcome, Junkyard Boy, to your new home.

Chapter THREE

YOU THINK THERE'S A FRONT YARD? There's not. It's all junk-yard. To get to the front door, you got to drive through stacks of old tires, some taller than me, taller than my daddy even. There's piles of rusty car doors, hoods, broken-down trailers, hubcaps wired to a chain-link fence, piles of radiators, car grills, wheels—some fancy chrome, some not—pieces of every kind of car which have been rained on, tore up, chipped, wrecked, and faded by the sun. Babe's got anything you want, plus plenty of stuff you don't want.

A sign wired to the chain-link fence in the front says you pay two dollars to go inside the yard, and you bring your own socket wrench to take off what you want. Another sign points to a spaceship made out of two hubcaps mounted on a pole. The sign says Metal Art for Sale. Daddy is in such an all-fired hurry that he pulls to a stop, jumps out, and slams his door. Today he is not looking for anything. He's found what he wants. Jewel. In only a few more minutes he can be on his way to get her. He's in such a rush that he's out of the truck and halfway to the door before he thinks about me.

I'm sitting in the truck, looking down at the duct tape covering all the rips in the front seat. Before we left home, I helped him tape up every single rip. My daddy don't want no springs poking his precious Jewel in the butt.

I can see her so clear in my mind. She's at Skate Ranch where she works, her skinny legs sticking out of her pink roller-skating skirt, her fuzzy blond hair, her sassy mouth telling me to have a free Coke and go play video games away from her and Daddy. Just thinking about Jewel makes me so mad, I can't think. I don't even notice that my fingers inch their way across the truck seat and grab the edge of a piece of duct tape. I tug on it just a little at first, then pull. It makes a slow r-r-r-r-rip. The next piece, I yank harder. It makes a giant pop as the end of the tape pulls away from the vinyl. I grab hold of another piece. It's easy. In only a few seconds I have stripped almost every piece of tape off the vinyl seat. Springs and stuffing are coming out everywhere.

You think I'm mean, full of the devil? Maybe I am. You think I'm scared about my daddy going off, about being left? I ain't no baby crying for his mama, for his daddy, neither. I ain't crying about nothing. But one thing I am. Mad.

Daddy's almost to the front door. He stops, turns

around, and looks back at the truck. Come on, he motions. He stands there a second looking at me. He's trying to figure out what to do. Finally, he walks back toward me. I lock the door.

He's coming closer, and it ain't hard to see what he's saying.

"Open it."

I am frozen, pretending I can't breathe, and in a way, I can't. My heart is sliding up to my throat. He's up close to the window now, and he sees the seat. He's pointing down where the stuffing pokes out in fuzzy white lines, and his eyebrows are twitching like they do when he's threatening to take off his belt and whop me. You think he's hit me before? Not yet, he hasn't, but this time, I figure he really might.

While he watches, I rip off the last piece of tape and throw it on the floorboard. This seat is now a royal mess.

He shoves his hand into his pocket and jerks out the keys. He jabs at the door lock and rips open the door.

"Get out!"

My feet don't want to move.

"I want to go to South Dakota with you," I holler.

"Out!" he hollers back, reaching to grab me. I scoot away from him at the last second.

"You got two choices, Matchit. Walk, or get carried. Which is it?" By now, he's got sweat rings big as Saturn under his arms, messing up his new shirt. I know he means business, and I slide out of the truck.

Soon as I hit the ground, I kick at the dirt as hard as I

19

can, so hard a cloud spirals up around my feet. I give the dirt another kick, harder this time. Daddy don't even notice. He's already up to the front steps. I kick the ground so hard and so fast, dirt swirls up around my face. It's thick as a cyclone, so thick I don't even see what I'm kicking. Then I feel something hard against my toe. Clang! Pop! I kick that hubcap so hard, it flies into the air, six, eight feet at least, maybe ten. That thing is sailing! Wh-iii-shh! It's heading straight for the back of my daddy's head.

I'm just about to holler when smack! An arm wearing a long-sleeved shirt that's just about made out of patches reaches out from behind a stack of tires and catches that hubcap midair.

Daddy spins around. "What's that?" He must've heard something, but he don't know he just about got clobbered.

A man wearing a funny cap with earflaps steps out. He's tall and wore-out looking, dried up as a piece of beef jerky. He wears work boots that are cracked across the toes, old denim overalls, and a long-sleeved shirt. Don't he know it's hot out here? That guy don't care nothing about how he looks. You can bet he don't shave. Everything grows wild around his lips. His beard runs down over his chin and spills onto his overalls like a dirty waterfall.

He don't look like he could catch nothing, but he's got the hubcap in his hand.

"This yours?" the man says to Daddy.

Daddy says no.

The guy looks straight at me. You can tell by the look in

his eyes that he saw me kick that hubcap. He's got me pinned to the wall with those eyes of his. I look down and hold my breath. I could be in big trouble. Again.

He sets the hubcap down on the ground.

"Is Babe inside?" Daddy asks.

The man nods and points to the door.

"Matchit," Daddy says, "come on."

I turn and look back at the man. He's watching me. I walk as slow as I can, following Daddy to a steering wheel mounted on a board at the front door. There's a sign that says Honk and Come In.

"You want to honk the horn?"

I shake my head. Any other day, I would like to do that part, but not today. Today is the day I'm about to get left at a junkyard. My hands are shaking. My heart is running wild inside my chest.

Daddy sets my suitcase down in the dirt next to the front steps. He takes out his handkerchief and wipes the sweat off his face. It's time to go inside.

"Ready?" Daddy asks. And without waiting for me to answer, he honks the horn on the steering wheel two times, and pushes open the screen door.

Chapter FOUR

BABE IS SITTING ON A BAR STOOL AT THE COUNTER playing solitaire. She's wrapped in a wad of cigar smoke.

"Howdy, Miss America!" Daddy says as he stands inside the doorway.

She looks up.

Babe ain't hardly Miss America. She's got sweat splotched around the neck of her T-shirt, drips of sweat streaking down the sides of her face, which is not skinny, far from it. She's got sweat even shining on her arms. Plus she's got a cigar in her mouth.

"Who are you?" She squints at us, and when she can't make nothing out, she reaches for a pair of eyeglasses sitting next to her ashtray and puts them on.

"Arnie McCarty," Daddy says. "Remember me? That job down in Houston? Ten years ago?" He sounds worried. He's hoping so bad she'll remember. "Arnie," he repeats.

"The one with the baby?"

"He's not a baby anymore," he says. He looks back at me.

She grins and puts down her cigar. I feel like I got a bat flying around in my stomach.

"I sure do remember you," she says. Daddy reaches for her hand, but she skips that, stands up, comes around the counter, and gives him a hug.

"It's good to see you, Arnie. Real good. You're cute as ever. And this must be your baby."

I am behind Daddy. I ain't in no hurry to shake nobody's hand or get hugged. And I ain't no baby.

"It's him," Daddy says. "He's all grown up. We thought we'd drive out and see your place." He stutters and glances down at his feet.

My daddy don't even tell a lie good.

I look around. This place is oily and the counter is dirty. The air stinks. Also, it's sweltering hot and crowded in this front room. It's too small and there's too many old greasy car parts stacked on the floor, on shelves, the counter, everywhere you can see. There's a ceiling fan trying to stir up the air, but it don't do no good.

Daddy takes a loud sniff and says the place smells better than Mrs. Baird's Bread Factory. He is one liar. This room is full of cigar smoke and something that smells like rubber and oil, like plastic fishing worms, only worse.

I hang back at the door, next to a shelf full of distributor plugs. They are stiff dead things, black wires sprouting out like spider legs. There's boxes of starters, alternators, all kinds of plugs, broken axles, used-up brake drums, and transmissions that's been pulled out of wrecked cars. She's got grills hanging from the ceiling, red taillights hung in lines up and down the walls, old Texas license plates nailed in a pattern to look like the state of Texas, and parts of the insides and outsides of cars piled up everywhere.

My brain says Matchit, this is where you're going to have to stay. Look at all these crashed cars. They get dragged in, hooked on chains, they get gutted like fish, their insides tore out, the good parts put on a shelf or in a box. What's left gets stuck out in the yard or taken to the metal-processing plant where they get smashed and melted down. They don't have no choice what happens to them. All the sudden I feel soft inside, like something broke loose. I press my back teeth together and squeeze my eyes shut. I take a deep breath.

Daddy shoots the bull awhile, talking about wheel covers and chrome bumpers. Then he launches right into what he's come for, telling Babe how things are rough in the construction business these days, how he has to take jobs out of town, how something suddenly came up. He don't have no place to leave me.

"I hate to take Matchit with me because he'd be spending too much time unsupervised," he says. Then he tells how his cousin Jake was going to keep me, but he got called out of town on an emergency, which I know means the car races. And how my mother has been detained, and

24

I don't know what he means by that word, but I don't think he's told the truth about her, either. I don't say nothing, though.

"Matchit thinks he can stay by himself being it's just a few days," he says. "Shoot, he's a real mature kid, but I don't like the idea. You never know what could happen even if it is for a short time."

I figure Daddy knows good and well it might not be a short time. It could be a whole lot longer or it could be shorter. It all depends. He don't say what it depends on, but I know.

Babe gathers up her cards and shuffles them. She takes the bait, smooth as can be.

"You leave that boy here with me. We can get by just fine."

Daddy acts like he never thought of the idea before. He looks down and fiddles with the wallet chain hanging from his belt. "That'd cause too much trouble," he says real soft, glancing back at me.

"Shoot, he won't hurt nothing," Babe says, setting her cards on the counter and her cigar in the ashtray in front of her. So my daddy agrees. He picks up the king of diamonds and holds it in front of his mouth while he lowers his voice, but I hear what he's saying, "I'll give you my cousin Jake's number. He usually keeps Match. In a couple of days he can come get him."

"I ain't staying with Jake!" I say it loud enough for them both to hear.

I mean it. I've had it with Jake the Jerk. He thinks it's funny to pick you up by one belt loop and swing you around the room. It's funny to give you a brain tornado, which means he sneaks up behind you and scrubs the top of your head with his knuckles, then he says the same old thing: "You play with Barbie dolls, don't you?" Next, he wraps his fingers around the top of your arm to prove to anybody who's looking how skinny you are. Just the name Jake makes me feel like kicking somebody.

Daddy looks at his watch again. He's running late, and Jewel's going to be fuming mad. He rushes with what he's got to say, telling Babe all the things I can do to help her out: sweep the floor, wait on customers, wash dishes, do laundry. He slips her a twenty-dollar bill and says he'll send more. I'm thinking, don't count on nothing. I don't say it, though. She'll find out soon enough.

Babe picks up her cigar and takes a long drag. "Don't you worry," she says to Daddy, "me and Matchit, we'll be fine."

Daddy's shoulders relax. His plan worked, and he is so relieved. It is time for good-bye and the McCarty handshake, which only us two know. You make a fist, and then it's a bump, his fist on top of mine, then mine on his, then two bumps to the side. We do it the same way every single time. First we say good-bye, then there's the shake. Always.

This time, I have decided that I will put my hands in my pockets. I will turn my back, make him feel like a rat.

Daddy turns from Babe and heads toward me. I shove

my hands in my pockets and am just about to turn my back, but he don't notice. He rushes right past me.

The last thing I see before Daddy drives off is his grin. He figures he'll be back to get me.

He just don't know when.

Chapter *FIVE*

MATCHIT, YOU GOT THE LUCKIEST NAME IN THE WORLD.

That's what my daddy says, but don't you believe it. And don't look in one of those big fat books that has all the names in the universe printed in alphabetical order. It ain't there.

My name goes all the way back to when my mama's water broke, which Daddy sees as something all prettied up like that picture of Niagara Falls in my geography book at school.

The day I was born Daddy was playing poker. All his friends were talking, laughing, eating Fritos and bean dip, not paying no attention to nothing. Suddenly Mama sprung a leak. She hollered if somebody didn't stop playing cards and take her to the hospital, she was going to get up on the kitchen table and have me right there.

Jake slapped down his money and said to Daddy, fold or

match it. Mama, she was screaming by now. She wanted Daddy to get up from the table. The water that'd been holding me in so safe was coming out like a busted radiator hose. Still, Daddy didn't want to put his cards down. He said he couldn't fold on account of a lucky feeling inside him. He said to her, "Wait a minute." To Jake, he said, "I ain't folding. I'll match it!"

Daddy's cards turned out better than everybody else's and he won the whole pot. He got Mama to the hospital and they both ended up being glad about the money. And me, I got my name. Matchit. I've heard the story a million times about how lucky I am.

Daddy, he don't know nothing.

It wasn't long after I was born that Mama left. She didn't say good-bye to nobody. Daddy said I was one colicky baby, screaming my head off day and night. He said he walked me back and forth until the morning showed under the door and it was time for him to go to work. Mama couldn't take it. You call that luck?

Sure, I've visited my mama, but not in a long time. For most of my life it's just been me and Daddy and all his worries. And he's got plenty.

Every night, nearly, he sinks down into the sofa. He runs his hands through his hair, and names them all: groceries to buy, clothes to haul to the coin-operated laundry downstairs and carry back up again, bills to pay, jobs to find, but mostly he's got problems he don't know what to do with. He's got a kid that gets in fights every day nearly, a stack of papers with failing grades that he has to sign every Friday, behavior reports he's got to check and put his name on each one, and a list of teachers he's supposed to call. He's got notices on yellow paper that say Matchit McCarty's parents need to report to the assistant principal's office. Matchit McCarty's parents need to call the school counselor, need to call the school testing lady, even need to call the lady on the register in the cafeteria. There's no way my daddy can stay on top of it all. He says he feels like he slipped and fell into a ditch of snakes.

Then he met Jewel.

It was on Halloween at the All-School Skating Party, the worst night of my life. Jake the Jerk, the second cousin I don't claim, loves to tell about it. Every time we eat at Burger Barn, he starts in. He sits down with his double order of double-large French fries and double chocolate shake and says real loud, "I'll never forget Halloween at the skating rink." When he's sure the pretty girl at the counter is listening, he'll go on.

"Me and Arnie come in the door at Skate Ranch to pick up Matchit. So we can't find him at first. We're looking all around the skate floor for him. And we seen a bunch of ghosts on skates, some werewolves, about fifty ballerinas, and space aliens, they're all over the place. So Arnie turns around and says to me, 'You see a Dracula anywhere?' "

At this part in the story, Jake starts laughing, and before he quits, he just about got milk shake pouring out his nose. "So we're looking around," he says. "Then we both see him. Dracula is way over at the edge of the rink, grab-

30

straight into his. "Your buddy, I think, left this next to the cash register when he paid for his food. My name is Jewel."

Daddy said thanks, but that wasn't the end of it. He couldn't take his eyes off her. He stood there all goofy-faced, stuttering around about what a nice roller rink they got, how she skates so good, how this has been a great party, and a whole lot of other big fat lies. Jewel agreed with everything he said, and for a minute both of them just stood there looking at each other.

"Well, I better go," she said. She handed Daddy the bill-fold, and it dropped on the floor between them. She bent over to pick it up, and Daddy about broke his neck trying to get to it first. Part of her body bumped onto his, and she giggled.

Daddy froze. You'd think he just got struck by lightning. He couldn't even talk, hardly.

Finally, she said good-bye and skated off. He was watching her the whole way.

"Matchit," he said, "that woman can flash a smile as bright as a welcome light on a motel at night."

Right at that minute Jewel got stuck on his brain like one of those tattoo decals. You can't ever get them things off. That's when my life got a million times unluckier.

Chapter SIX

AFTER DADDY FORGETS TO SAY GOOD-BYE and climbs in his truck, he's in such a hurry to get Jewel, he peels out from Babe's drive, and if it had been paved, he'd have left some rubber, I'm sure. Me, I sit down with my suitcase outside on the bottom porch step. I'm thinking I might sit right here until he comes back. I might not eat, sleep, nothing. I might die of hunger or thirst, or get one of those diseases you get when mosquitoes bite you too much. I don't care what happens. It would serve him right to see his son shriveled up and dead on the porch when he drives back.

The only thing is, it is hot out here, over one hundred degrees probably. The sun is beating down on me. I feel the sweat running down my legs inside my jeans. New jeans are always hotter than old ones, and these are the worst. There ain't a tree in sight, and it probably hasn't rained in a year. There are cracks in the ground big enough to put your hand inside.

Just thinking how Daddy took off makes my fist smash down on the top of my suitcase so hard, the hurt crawls up my wrist and runs back down to the tip of my little finger. I feel the tears crowd up in my eyes, and just in case, I cover my face. I'd like to kick somebody, but I ain't going to cry.

My brain says You feel better, Matchstick? Now that you got a sore hand?

Mind your own business, I grumble under my breath. I don't feel better or worse. I am a hole in the sky. I don't feel nothing.

Babe pokes her head out the door. "You still outside?" she asks. She knows good and well I haven't gone nowhere.

She walks down the steps and stands in the dirt beside me. "Are you sure I can't bring you something? Iced tea? Iced coffee?" She slaps her forehead. "What am I think-ing? Boys your age like root beer, RC, drinks like that. Chocolate milk. I don't have any of those things. We need to go to the grocery store. You like to go grocery shop-ping?"

"Not really," I mumble. I don't even look at her.

She laughs loud enough to wake up the dead. What did I say that was so funny? I don't believe this woman. She ought to laugh at her own self. She's the one got chopped-up gray hair like Moe on the Three Stooges.

"I'm not sure what a boy likes to do. Taking on a child

has never been in my range of thought," she says. "Cars I know. Give me a kid and I don't even know how to open the hood." She laughs again, full and long, like thunder that don't want to stop. Keeping me is the funniest joke in the universe.

"Did you see that?" She points to some kind of crazy-looking statue that's standing at the corner of the house. It's about three feet tall and it's made out of all kinds of car parts, door handles, fan blades, I don't know what all. It looks like an alien. "He was made by an artist," she says, walking over to it. There's a shooter marble in the creature's hand. She picks it up, puts it in his mouth, and it rolls down a maze that comes out one of his toes. "Isn't he cute?"

She's expecting me to smile. But I don't.

She sits down on an old tractor tire by the steps and starts talking. That woman don't know when to quit. She talks about how happy she is she got company for a change. first time since somebody died nearly, except for every New Year's Eve when she throws a huge party for everybody who wants to come, and then there's Sister (who, by the way, is not her real sister, she tells me), and who owns the taxidermy down the road, but she's not exactly company be-cause she visits all the time. Also there's a few people who come to the yard looking to buy turn signals or rear ends, things like that. Sometimes they buy yard art like the statue she showed me. These customers sometimes visit for a while, but they aren't really company. And she does have Zebby. He's the artist. He lives in the school bus on the edge of the yard, but he don't like to talk much. Besides, he's been here too long to be called company.

Zebby? He must have been the weird guy who caught that hubcap. He didn't look like no artist. Artists don't wear caps with earflaps.

She starts telling me all about Zebby whether I care to listen or not. He sells the metal art advertised on the sign out front. She can't say enough about how smart he is. His name, Zebedee, comes out of the holy Bible, she says. He must be smart. The Bible Zebedee was a fisherman. She goes on and on until after a while, I don't know which Zebby she's talking about, the artist or the fisherman, so I tune out, which is something I learned at school.

I'm not thinking about nothing, then I hear one line. "And he sewed up his own leg," she says. Now that gets my attention. I look over at her.

"It happened last fall when he was cutting some sheet metal. His hand slipped and he sliced the inside of his thigh. He came up to the house to wash it, and I just about fainted. I wanted to take him into town to get a tetanus shot and stitches, but he wouldn't have it. He said he'd had a tetanus shot, and he wasn't going to pay someone to sew up his leg. He'd do it himself."

I can't believe it. That guy don't look like he could squash a flea.

"Anyway, Matchit. Don't go out by Zebby's bus. He can't be bothered while he's working. He's a sculptor. Do you know what a sculptor is, Matchit?"

I roll my eyes on that. Does she think she's playing

37

school or what? Of course I know the answer to that question. A soap dish would know what a sculptor is.

Back when Hercules lived, they had sculptors all over the place. Mostly they carved naked people out of rock.

"Right now Zebedee's working on a big important sculpture out by the scaffold next to his bus. He uses car bumpers, fenders, and other wrecked parts of cars."

You kidding me? That guy think he can make a naked woman out of car bumpers? I doubt it.

Babe keeps talking, a mile a minute. She says Zebedee has been working on this particular sculpture for a year, but no matter how hard he works, he can't seem to get it right. All day and half the night he's working on it, but he keeps tearing it up and starting over.

All sculptors have to do is use their hands. His seemed okay to me. They caught that hubcap real good. Daddy almost got hit in the head, but he never even knew it. You can bet he's not paying attention to nothing now, either, except for Jewel. She's probably already kicked off her high heels and is hanging her feet out the window. She's probably leaning against Daddy, her head on his shoulder. He probably can't even shift gears, hardly.

I look at my own hands. The one I smashed on top of the suitcase is turning blue along the edge of my palm, and I wish it would be broken, and I wish that a broken-off sliver of bone might ride up to my heart and we'd have to call 911. Daddy would be good and sorry he ever left without me.

Babe keeps talking. She says she is so proud and lucky

to finally have a kid around the place. She always wanted one. I'm scared for a minute she's going to hug me. I scoot over a few inches, holding my sore hand in my lap.

I don't want nobody hugging me.

Plus I'm not her kid. I don't like her thinking I am. I give her a dirty look, but she don't even notice. She just grins. "Let's go to the grocery store, sugar."

I feel my face overheat and nearly boil over, her calling me baby names like that.

"I think I'll stay here on the steps," I tell her. I'm hoping hoping hoping Daddy has changed his mind. I am hoping Jewel got mad and got herself on a Greyhound bus, and he's headed back to the junkyard.

"Well, I'll just stay with you," Babe says. She gets up from the tractor tire where she's been sitting and comes over to the steps. She sits down next to me and says, "I'll keep you company."

I'm frowning like crazy, but she don't seem to even notice.

"What grade are you in?" she asks. "You're in the smart class, I can tell that."

She don't know beans. If you're in Gifted and Talented, you're in the smart class. You go on field trips to the Community Center to eat breakfast with the mayor, and you have to count in Japanese, and you get to touch a sheep's brain. GT kids have to hold the school doors open when the superintendent visits, and they got to write a book report on every book in the library. You think I'm in that class? You're wrong.

About my grade, I say seventh. That's what I'm hoping.

I don't tell her about the letter that says come to a meeting at the start of the new school year. Come see if you belong in Slow and Dumb.

At school my brain don't pay one bit of attention. Half the time it pretends it's a monster scorpion with a stinger three feet long. It crawls around the room knocking pencils off people's desks. It brags Nobody can make me read, spell, do math. Sometimes it curls up and goes to sleep, but you better not touch it. You'll be sorry.

You think I got that attention defeated disease? I been asked that question plenty. Matchit McCarty, you don't got no diseases. You're downright loony, I tell myself. Where you really belong is ED class. I heard kids in Emotional Dumb stay in a gray-and-brown temporary building out by the gym. They don't mix with the rest of the school. When it comes time for lunch, a cafeteria lady in a pink dress and white nurse shoes wheels the lunch cart out there so that they can eat. These kids are all messed up. They don't know whether to laugh, cry, or scream. Pee in their pants half the time. That's what I heard.

"You drive yet?" It's Babe.

What? You crazy? You dumb? My brain thinks it got stuck in a house with Dumb Ed. I shake my head about the driving. This lady don't know nothing about kids.

"Okay, then, I'll take the wheel," she says, laughing again. "You want to ride in the Mustang?" She tells me it's a 1964½ with original blue paint, chrome hubcaps, 289 automatic, bucket seats, the works.

Daddy would love a car like that. I wish he could've

heard Babe ask me if I wanted to drive it. He wouldn't believe his ears.

She stands up and tells me to follow her. The car is parked in a shed about fifty feet from the side of the house, and on our way out there I look out and see that crazy guy's school bus over on the edge of the yard. I can see part of his sculpture leaning against the bus. It ain't nothing. Just a bunch of wrecked car parts stuck together.

Babe's telling me how she's got a bunch of pet pigeons that hang around, which is part of the reason she keeps the car in a shed. "I love those birds," she says, "but I don't want them messing with my car." She is proud about that car, and I would be, too.

The Mustang is in pretty good condition on the outside, but not so good on the inside. She's explaining how she's still got quite a bit of work to do before it's totally fixed up. "Wait until you see Sister's car," she says. "Her seats look brand new, not like these old things."

I look in the passenger seat window. Babe's got duct tape covering the rips in her seat, just like our truck. "Go ahead, get in," she says, and I open the door and slide inside, sitting down on the crisscross lines of tape, which reminds me of our truck, my daddy's and mine. Suddenly, my brain's got me by the throat. It's squeezing until I feel my eyes water up.

Matchstick, you big baby, you going to cry in front of this lady?

No, I ain't. My fingernails squeeze into my fist so hard, I have to check to make sure blood didn't come out my palm. I wish I could beat up somebody. I would do it. But there ain't no one here, just me and Babe.

"Go ahead, shut the door," Babe says. I slam that thing so hard, you could hear it for a mile, I bet. Babe, she laughs. She says I got the strength of Samson. "You going to fight an army with a jawbone?"

Huh? That woman don't make no sense. Besides, she got fuzzy dice hanging from her mirror, a stuffed yellow tiger in the back window, magnets stuck everywhere, on the dashboard, on the outside of the glove compartment. Most have sayings like Don't Worry, Have Fun, and I Ain't Fat, I'm Cuddly. She's messed up the interior of this car something fierce. My daddy and I could fix it up good. Right now, this car ain't nothing but a carnival on wheels.

"I knew it," she says, starting the engine. "Sister and I rebuilt the master cylinder on this thing, replaced the rest of the original front suspension, but these seats. I knew I should have got me some new seats. Now company is here and I got these old ripped-up things. You think I wouldn't be that lazy!" She laughs at herself the whole time we're dodging potholes in the road.

Chapter SEVEN

THIS TOWN'S GOT NO APARTMENT COMPLEXES. All it's got is satellite dishes and clotheslines in the backyards. Seems like everybody got white T-shirts and white sheets hanging on the lines in this town. And nobody's outside. It's too hot.

When we get to Taylor's Grocery, Babe says she hopes she runs into someone she knows, so she can show off her new company, but the store is nearly empty. She has to make do with Al. He's behind the meat counter grinding up hamburger. He's got piles of hamburger sitting everywhere back there. She asks him if he has any knucklebones because she got a stray dog that stops by the house sometimes. "When Freebie comes by, I don't have anything good to offer him," she says, laughing.

Al steps around from behind the grinder, rubbing his bloody hands on his white apron.

"This woman feeds anything that comes on her property," he says to me. "She feeding you?"

I don't know what to say. I ain't ate nothing yet.

Babe stiffens. "What about the knucklebones?" she reminds him.

"I got a whole femur," he says, and while he wraps it up in butcher paper, he asks about me. "Who you got there, another artist friend?" I feel him looking at me.

Babe says, "This is Matchit. He's my company. I don't know if he's an artist or not. Probably is. He's in the Gifted and Talented Class."

This woman is crazy with a capital *C*. Daddy would say she is one brick short of a load. Al, the butcher, smiles at me. "You say Matchit? What kind of name is that?" My name is a story I don't feel like explaining. I shrug my shoulders.

Babe don't care if I answer or if I don't. She laughs and grabs a grocery cart, not just a hand-carry basket. First thing she does, after she drops the bone in the cart with a plunk, is cut a wheelie to the milk section. She expect me to follow her that fast?

"Come on, I need your help," she hollers from across the store. This woman is embarrassing. My brain says You going to let her make a fool out of you?

No, I ain't. I ain't running across the store for nobody. I barely move in the direction of her voice, kicking at the shiny floor with my toes. It makes a squeak squeak squeak. I ain't in no hurry.

When I finally get to the dairy case, she asks, "You like

chocolate milk? All the commercials show kids drinking it." She don't wait for an answer. She hands me two half-gallon cartons. Don't she know the powdered mix is a whole lot cheaper and lasts longer? But no, that won't do, she's got to have the real thing. I set the milk down in the bottom of the cart next to the leg bone, and she hands me two more cartons.

"You think that will be enough?" she asks. That woman, she *is* crazy.

"Oatmeal!" Babe announces. She's put on funny little halfway glasses and she is reading off the back of the tallest oatmeal box I've ever seen. I don't like the stuff. Me and Daddy eat Pop-Tarts for breakfast. Only people without teeth eat soft hot cereal.

"Matchit," she says, "we'll make us some cookies. Every TV show I ever saw with kids on it has cookies." She reads aloud the chocolate chip cookie recipe on the back of the oatmeal box. Then she starts telling me what to do. Run get a five-pound bag of sugar. Run get flour. We got to have large brown eggs, not medium white, we got to have baking soda, the one in the yellow box, and we got to have vanilla. She can't decide if the recipe means vanilla extract, vanilla flavoring, or vanilla beans. Do we want raisins and chocolate chips? Pecans or no nuts at all? When we go for the chocolate, there's milk chocolate, semisweet, small morsels and large. With the nuts you got to choose crushed or broken, halves or in the shell. She reads all the packages, trying to decide. Finally, she takes some of everything. There are decisions about whether to choose butter, oleo, or Crisco, dark brown sugar or light. Babe laughs and says she never knew how downright complicated cookies could be.

That's why me and Daddy buy cookie dough in a package. You slice it, you cook it, and you eat it. One night during Court TV, we baked a whole package and ate every single cookie. Then Jewel came over. She ruined everything, like always. She scooted up next to Daddy on the couch. He started laughing at everything she said, no matter how dumb. "You have the sweetest fingers," she said. And she kissed his fingernails, one through ten. Right now, I bet that's what she's doing.

"You coming, Matchit?"

Babe's pushing the grocery cart up and down the aisles like she got a plan. She's looking over everything. "Matchit, do kids like this?" She holds up a box of graham crackers. Do they like these? Cheese crackers. That woman tosses boxes in the basket like there ain't no tomorrow.

The whole time she's explaining. Her oven is chockfull of car parts, she tells me, but she'll clean it out and figure how to turn it on. The pantry's loaded up with tools, but she'll clean that out, too. A boy's got to have lots of snacks. He needs homemade cookies, not store-bought, fresh fruit, salted peanuts in the shells, healthy granola cereal, and sugar cereal for snacks. All down the aisles, she laughs at everything, the way I wrinkle up my face when she shows me a jar of pickled pigs' feet, the way an eggplant looks. She tells me we might make spaghetti squash. Have I ever had that? And we might make S'mores, which means we got to have big marshmallows and Hershey bars. She laughs about how a lady her age ought to know how to cook, ought to know how to raise a child. And on the way out, she picks up a paperback book from the rack next to the cash register: *How to Raise a Kid in Ten Easy Lessons.*

That woman got Looney Tunes in her head. I'm practically already raised. Besides, I don't need no mama.

Babe asks me to help her load everything into the trunk. After that, she buys three Big Reds from the Coke machine outside the store, one for each of us and one to take home to Zebby.

"Matchit," Babe begins as we sit in the car inside the parking lot. She runs her fingers through her gray spiky hair. "I've never been a parent, but I sure do want to try." I want to tell her that the first thing she should do is put out her cigar, on account of secondhand smoke. I don't say anything, though.

I've been around worse.

Chapter EIGHT

WHEN BABE'S PUTTING UP THE GROCERIES, she asks me if I stay with my mother very often. I say no.

Why? She wants to know.

I don't answer, I just shrug my shoulders. The last time I stayed a few days with my mother, she forgot to buy bread, forgot to buy milk, forgot to put sheets on my bed. She even forgot to take me to school. Then when Daddy came to get me, she cried and carried on like she'd taken care of me my whole life. She stood outside the door of her apartment on the second floor, leaning over the railing, hollering at my daddy and at me, at the drainpipes on the roof, at the cars in the parking lot, anything. I wanted to turn around and look, but Daddy said keep going straight ahead, Matchit. Hurry up. Still, I took one peek back. Her blouse was buttoned wrong and a pink hair roller hung from one piece of hair like it wanted to let go. She had a scared look on her face.

Daddy got me by the arm and he said, "Dang it, Matchit. Come on. I should've never left you here." We were going down the fire-escape stairs because they were closer than the main stairway, and the whole time Mama was crying about how she counted the creases in my legs and arms the day I was born, that there were seventeen and she even wrote it down on the back of the gas station receipt that they got on the way home from the hospital. She figured that was proof enough for anyone of how much she cared.

So why did she leave us in the first place? Ain't nobody knows the answer to that. She left. That's all that matters. Daddy says when it comes to raising a kid, it takes more than emotion. My mama don't even got that right. She's Emotional Dumb. She wants me and she don't want me. And that's the problem. My mama can't make up her mind about nothing. Her mind is a load of towels that ain't been folded.

"Matchit?" Babe says, setting a bag of marshmallows on the table. "You didn't answer me. Why can't you stay with your mother?"

"At my mama's place, there's not much room," I answer.

At home, Daddy and I both sleep in the living room because what we have is called an efficiency apartment. He gets the bed that pulls out of the wall. I get the sofa across from the TV. It's enough.

Babe can't think where in her house she is going to put me because she doesn't have much space. But she has got to figure out where I'm going to sleep. Her house is not very big, and most of it is full of car parts. Her face scrunches up in a worried look. There's the front room, but that's where people come in to pay for their parts. You can't hardly see for all the junk, and you can't walk without stepping on something.

After the front room, there's the kitchen. The table's even filled up with junk, old bolts, tools, and hood ornaments. Cleaned up, it still wouldn't be that good, not for a kid to sleep in, she says. There's one bathroom, and it's small. I can sleep in the tub, I say, it won't be long before my daddy gets me, anyway. Plus, I've done it before, once at Jake's. Kept the door locked all night long.

But she won't have it.

Babe's got two bedrooms, one for her and one for inventory, which is stacked to the ceiling. She's got spare car parts, mufflers, radiators, carburetors, and prize items such as wooden steering wheels and fancy gearshift knobs. She says it'd take a century to move all that stuff so I could have the room to myself. She wishes she had a nice guest house, or at least a nice guest room with a bed and comforter and a chest of drawers. Since she don't have that, she wishes she at least had a big walk-in closet that would be large enough for a cot.

Babe's at her little finger, counting off all the places she don't have. She don't have a couch with a bed inside, she don't have a study where you could add a bed, she don't have a special room. She don't have a nice living room with a big soft chair. She's shaking her head.

I say I can sleep anywhere. I've slept in a tent in the mountains. I could sleep outside, on the porch, even. At that one her eyes light up.

"That's it, Matchit. The back porch!"

She tells me to follow her to the very back of the house, behind the kitchen. The screened-in porch is long and narrow, but it's pretty big. You can look out and see the whole junkyard, all the way out to the school bus on the edge of the yard. Babe says her friend, Sister, has a roll-away bed that will do. She apologizes that the floor is concrete, and nothing is painted, but that's okay with me. Also, there's quite a bit of junk in there, a couple of barbecue grills, an old wooden porch swing, and lots of other things. But Babe says all that stuff can be moved outside. "Do you think you would mind having this room?" she asks.

I don't mind. It's only for a few days. It's screened in so the mosquitoes can't chew on me, and no snakes can get in. The room has got to be cleaned up, sure, but it'll do. Three sides of the room are nothing but screens looking out over the junkyard, but I don't mind about that. The wind can blow through the screens and cool me off, and at night if it's not cloudy, I might be able to look outside and see the Big Dipper. It'd be like sleeping outside in the mountains, only instead of mountains and trees, there's cars.

But there is one thing. What if it rains?

Don't worry, Babe says, she's got tarps mounted above the screens. I can roll them down if I want.

It'll be just like a tent.

Still, Babe is worried. Chapter One of her raising kids book is titled "A Child Needs His or Her Own Space."

Space—does that mean a place to sleep? Or is it a place to hang out?

She don't think the porch is good enough. It's okay for sleeping, but it's not so good for hanging out. "What will we do?" she says out loud.

By the next morning she's figured it out.

Chapter
NINE

"HOW WOULD YOU LIKE TO HAVE YOUR OWN VAN? Not to sleep in, of course, but just to have your own private place."

Huh? I look up. What does she mean, my own?

"There's an old Dodge van sitting out in the yard. What do you think?"

I don't do nothing but shrug my shoulders, but inside I feel a little excited.

"You can fix it up yourself, however you like," she says. "Want to see it?"

She says to follow her, and I do because I don't have anything else to do, and I am a little bit curious.

We have to walk past a lot of broken-down cars, old Chevrolets, Fords, Dodges, and a bunch of others. There's even two old Thunderbirds. Man, you haven't seen Thunderbirds like that on the road for a hundred years, well, maybe not that long, but it was in the old days, I know that. Most of these cars got their bumpers missing, grills, hood ornaments, wheels, you name it. There ain't nothing left but shells on some of these cars. Some, though, don't look that bad.

Babe explains how the car business is bad. "People don't fix up their cars like they used to," she says. "First there's technology—too much electronics—and then there's computer chips. People don't know how to fix things like that, and they can't find what they need in a junkyard. If they wreck their cars, and the damage is not too bad, they just pick up their insurance check and go on. They have to buy groceries, you know. Or they just get rid of the car and start over. It's a throwaway world. That's how things go today—got a problem, throw it out and start over."

My brain says Boy, you been a problem since the day you was born. Now your daddy got a chance to start over. He threw you in the dump where you belong.

"Shut up," I mumble.

"What?" Babe asks.

"Not you," I say, feeling a little embarrassed.

She laughs and tells me there's a lot of times she does need to shut up. And to go ahead, tell her. This woman, she thinks backwards. If she was at my school, she'd get sent to the testing center.

The van is not what you'd call fresh. It used to be white, but now it's the color of dirty bathwater.

Babe kicks at the wheels, which are sunk into a foot of weeds.

Inside, the door panels are missing except for one in the back, and the seats are gone, too, except for the driver's, but that just gives it more room. Somehow you could fix up a light. It's got unbroken windows along both sides, and an unbroken windshield in the front, so ain't nothing going to be crawling in. A person could live in a van.

I look across the yard at Zebby's school bus. No way I'd live in one of those. It's bad enough to ride in one.

Babe says, "I've got a battery-operated fan you could use so it won't be so hot. And I've got a light you can have. If you like it, it's all yours, Matchit."

Mine? I don't know if she's telling me the truth or not. "Will it still drive?" I ask.

She pushes her unlit cigar to the corner of her mouth and studies the van. "Might could. It needs some work, an engine for one thing. Tell you the truth, most everything's missing under the hood."

Still, it's a van. And it's mine. Babe gives me three old license plates, one Colorado with a little purple mountain on it, one New York with a Statue of Liberty, and one Texas, white with a red, white, and blue Texas flag. She says I can decorate my own place anyway I like, come out here anytime I want. And the light she gives me has three switches, red, white, and green. I can rig that thing up really good. Anything I find in my old van, I can keep, even money.

"Have at it!" she says, opening the door on the driver's side. "You might want some time to yourself." I climb in and sit down, and she goes back inside the house.

This place is all mine. I run my hands over the dash. It ain't even cracked. It's hot inside, and smells like an old tennis shoe, but this van is in pretty good shape. The glove compartment comes right open, you don't even have to tug at it, and it's still full of stuff. First, there's a map of the United States. Somebody marked a blue line all the way from New York to California, or maybe it's the other way around. I don't know, but somebody was going someplace, I know that. There's a lot of old yellow receipts, Taco Palace, Burger Bar, Dairy Queen. Those I pull out to throw away later. There's a manual, too. It shows pictures about how to change the oil, change a tire, check the fuses for windshield wipers. There's not any windshield wipers, but they can be replaced, I bet. This book I'm keeping. It'll come in handy.

Next, I reach into the back of the compartment. There's a plastic hair clip with a pink bow. I don't need that. There's an empty film box, an empty aspirin bottle, old lottery tickets, and a wooden coin that says Right on one side, Wrong on the other. I don't care about none of that stuff. My brain says What are you thinking, Matchit? Somebody left something good in here just for you? I ain't thinking that. I pick up all the trash and stuff it back in for now. I'm shoving the receipts back in, I feel something. It's one of those magnet boxes that holds a key, stuck up on the top of the compartment.

I know there won't be nothing. Or maybe just an old key for a van that don't work. Still, I pull it out and slide open the lid. Inside is a buffalo nickel. This old broken-down van showed me a good secret after all. I look out across the yard, see if anyone's looking.

The only person outside is Zebby and he's way out by his bus fooling with that piece of junk he's building. He ain't paying attention to me or nobody.

I crawl to the back, pry open the bottom corner of the door panel, and hide the key holder with the buffalo nickel. I ain't losing this.

I can think of a lot of things for this old van. I could build a tunnel going to it. I could make a secret code to use with the light Babe gave me, maybe find a battery radio. Maybe even paint this thing. Red. I could clean the inside, bring in a sleeping bag. I could camp out.

Then my brain starts talking to me. At first it's real soft, and then it gets louder. Hey, bad-luck boy, don't start making plans about no van. Do you think it's really yours? This van's just like the toys you used to play with at day care. Like a motel room. You go. It stays. This place is temporary. Besides, it's just a broken-down piece of junk.

I look around at all the stuff covering the floor, old yellow newspapers, crushed paper cups, pieces of trash people have shoved in here, and dirt, lots of dirt hardened on the floor like cement.

You dummy. You almost got excited about this old thing. My brain is right.

This van is pretty sorry if you ask me.

Chapter TEN

ONE WEEK GOES BY AND NO WORD FROM NOBODY. Then finally a call. They made it to Mount Rushmore, but right now Daddy's in a phone booth in Rapid City. He don't have to tell me that, I can tell from all the sounds of traffic. He's got news. Seems like Jewel suddenly remembered she got a couple of girlfriends living in a duplex up near Rapid City. After that brain explosion, she forgot all about the presidents carved in the side of the mountain.

"Mount Rushmore wasn't as great as Jewel thought it would be," he says. For a few seconds, we're both quiet. "I think she found something else she likes better."

"Another guy?"

"No. A dinosaur. They've got a huge green one built on one of the hills here. Jewel says she can see it out her bedroom window at her friends' place."

Suddenly, the whoosh of cars and a diesel putting on its brakes drowns out his voice.

"Daddy, you there?"

He says he is.

"Is Jewel hanging out with her friends instead of with you?"

"Well, yeah, I guess," he says.

He tries to explain that since she never got to stay in a college dormitory with a bunch of girls, she's making up for it.

"She tell you that?"

"Well, yes, she did. Sort of. But I think she's missed a lot of things in life, Matchit. She's trying to fill up some of those empty spots."

You got to fill up every hole you got inside you? It's just something I'm wondering, but I don't say it aloud.

"Where are you staying?"

"In the doghouse," my daddy says, like it's all one big joke.

"No, really, where are you?"

"Well, right now, I might try the YMCA. They have rooms you can rent on a temporary basis. Except, Match. I'm going to have to work for a couple of weeks. I need the money to get back home, but hey, there's good news." His voice tilts up, and he sounds like his old self again.

"I already found a job. Seventeen dollars an hour. Can you beat that with a stick?"

I'm not in the mood for jokes. "You said you'd go and be right back. I want you to come get me."

"I will," he says. "But I can't right now. I can't drag up on that job. Not yet, anyway. Tell Babe to call Jake."

I ignore that idea. "Did you send Babe any money? You said you would." Of course I already know what the answer is, but I want to get at him any way I can.

"I'm trying to tell you. I don't have it to send."

"Figures. What happened to the four hundred dollars?" There were four brand-new hundred-dollar bills lying on the dresser before we left.

"It's gone."

"You dropped the transmission?"

"The transmission's holding out. We lost a fan belt, though." He pauses, thinking what else he can say. "And," he finally continues, "I'm having to add oil every day. You know how much that costs. I can't help it, Matchit."

"I tried to tell you that old truck wouldn't make it. But oil and a fan belt don't cost four hundred dollars."

"I know it, Match. It just cost a lot of money to get here. I had to spend the cash on other things. You know."

"Jewel. I guess she ain't out of the picture yet," I say.

"Naw," he says. I can see him standing there with a worried look on his face, the telephone in one hand, the other hand rubbing the edge of one of his sideburns. He says, "I think when she settles down and sees how I'll stick by her through thick or thin, she'll come around, Matchit. She might be what you and me both been looking for."

Huh? I ain't been looking for no one.

The operator comes on to say Daddy owes another three dollars.

"Got to go, pal," he says.

Already? I don't even get to tell him about my room on the back porch, how the tarps pull down. How it reminds me of the tent we slept in on that camping trip in Colorado. How when I lie in bed, I almost hear the trout stream, the flip flip flip of the water hitting the rocks like fishes' tails. How I got a homesick feeling all over me.

My brain butts in. You're feeling homesick for something you never even had. You're crazy, boy.

"Matchit, you there?" Daddy's voice sounds a little worried.

"Where else?" I ask. I'm thinking about my van, how I might as well clean it up. It looks like I'm going to be staying here longer than I thought I would.

"I really gotta go. I'll call again soon. Don't worry," he says. Then he adds one more thing before he hangs up. "By the way, isn't somebody's birthday coming up? Whose is it? I forget," he teases.

My daddy always thinks he's a comedian. He's not.

"I hope somebody is thinking about what he wants for a present."

"Just come get me. That's all I want. I don't like it here. This lady calls me sugar."

Next thing I know, it's a dial tone.

Only one time my daddy forgot my birthday. Wait. He didn't forget. He was supposed to get paid, but he didn't. The job superintendent took off, didn't pay nobody. My daddy got so upset he couldn't come home. I don't blame him. Who could?

Next day, he says, "Matchit, when I come in last night, you'd fallen asleep with the SpaghettiOs can in your hand, the spoon was on the floor." And then my daddy put his head down on the kitchen table. It was my seventh birthday.

Afterwards, he swore come hay or high water, my birthday would not ever get missed again. And it never has. He wrote me a contract and signed it, drew a little rainbow by his name. My daddy said, "Remember how God signed his name on the sky with a rainbow? He promised no more floods to drown everything? Matchit, you ever hear of a flood that covered the whole earth again, every living thing drowned? A promise is a promise."

People do drown, I told him, maybe just not the whole world.

Chapter
ELEVEN

BABE WOULDN'T CALL ME SUGAR if she knew me at school. There I ain't one bit sweet.

I bet every teacher in the school building has heard stories about me. You can tell when I come in the first day. Their eyes are dreading what they see walking in the door. You're in my class? They got the desks lined up just right, everybody laid out in alphabetical order, clean pages in their grade book. All the lessons are mapped out. They've numbered all the things we're going to learn by Christmas. They got a chart with a goal set at the top, 100%. Uh-oh. They see me. They shake their heads. Nothing's going to go right in their world now.

One problem is teachers always start with the rules. They go on and on and on about this rule and that rule. Keep your hands and feet and other objects to yourself. Bring your supplies to class. Raise your hand when you want to speak. Stay on task. Do your homework. While they're explaining, they think I'm not listening to one word they're saying. I'm tapping on my desk with my pencil, tapping on my shoe, erasing the floor with my new eraser, seeing how many holes I can poke in a piece of notebook paper, zipping my notebook, unzipping my notebook, clicking my ballpoint pen open and shut. I'm drawing a picture on a piece of notebook paper.

They slam on the brakes.

You think you're so smart you don't have to listen, young man?

Everybody is laughing. Except the teacher. I'm going to call your mother, she warns. I'm laughing hard at that joke.

Go stand in the hall until you get serious about learning. You don't know when it's the right time to laugh, when it's time to be serious. What's wrong with you? You emotional dumb?

There's 483 ceiling tiles outside Mrs. White's language arts room. After the ceiling, I start counting light switches, classroom doors. I've been out there a lot of times. I ain't got serious yet.

Pretty soon the teacher files a report. She checks all the blanks about everything I don't do right. It's a lot of checks.

My teachers have been fed up with me for years. They don't know what to do. Last year, Mr. Samson, my science teacher, said, "Matchit, you bring your homework tomorrow, just one day, and I'll erase five zeroes in my grade book." Five! Only the next day, I couldn't find my paper. Mr. Samson said, "It figures."

"Shut up," I said. Well, not exactly. Not to the teacher. I said it to this boy named Nicholas who passed by me in the hall. He followed me into the classroom.

"You in my face, Matchstick?" he asked.

"If I want to be, I am."

All the sudden I saw green carpet. It slammed into my lips, and the taste of blood filled my mouth. I saw people's shoestrings and the bottoms of school desks stuck with gum. Everybody was hollering. There was a loud crack and it was my head. I rolled away from a desk leg, and we both grabbed and rolled, and I remembered how this same jerk wrote Matchstick with a red Sharpie on my locker door, and how he threw a roll of tape at me in art, and I dug the knuckles of one of my hands into his back as hard as I could. My other hand made a fist and I was about to plow into his stomach, but he hit me first, fast and sharp in the gut. I couldn't hardly breathe and about that time, I saw the teacher's knees and she was hollering for us to get up, and pretty soon somebody pulled us apart.

My nose was bleeding onto my collar, dripping red splotches on the front of my shirt. Nicholas was crying, hard and loud. Not me. Somebody hollered, "Get some paper towels out of the bathroom." I got an eye swelling up fast. One tooth felt loose, and my stomach hurt. I also got five days ISS. It doesn't matter one bit who starts a fight, which I think is unfair. It also doesn't matter who hits and who doesn't. You could stand there like a stick of butter and get the holy who beat out of you and you'd still get ISS. So you might as well fight. Nicholas, he got dragged to the other office.

Somebody said follow me, and I did because I was already in enough trouble. Next thing I knew, the door was shut behind me. I was in the AP's office. The assistant principal in charge of discipline read me the rules for In-School Suspension. They were the same ones the teacher read for the class, except there was an extra. You can't leave ISS for nothing, not even to go to the bathroom, unless it's a bathroom break where everybody lines up and the teacher in charge takes you. What if you want a drink of water? What if you get sick and have to go to the nurse? Forget it. You got to stay in ISS until your time is up, every hour, minute, and second of it, Bub.

After the AP was finished with all the rules, she told me to sign on the dotted line, then she scooted back in her chair and watched me. I bet she was trying to figure out how a kid who's littler than anybody except a couple of girls could get riled up enough to take on somebody twice as big. Finally, she said, "You have any questions, young man?"

I said, "Yeah. How old do you have to be to drop out of school?"

She said, "You have to be a lot of years past the sixth grade. Use your brain, Matchit, think about things before you act."

That's the problem. My brain don't pay no attention to me or anybody else. It looks at words on a page and scrambles them up like a bunch of eggs. It don't care about reading. Spelling, either. It don't care about nothing.

The teacher says, Matchit, spell *elevator* and letters come spilling out all kinds of ways, on top of each other like they're playing a big joke. Finally, my brain gets fed up. It marches up to some dude and says, "You think you're tough, don't you?"

The AP asked, "What do you plan to do when you grow up?"

I shrugged my shoulders.

"Is there anything you're interested in?" she asked.

I like to draw, but I didn't say it. It probably wasn't what she was looking for.

She said, "You need a vision for yourself, a dream. What is your dream, Mr. Matchit McCarty?"

I sat in the chair and said nothing.

Mostly, when summer comes, it's the best time for me. Except for now. This time I got dumped at the junkyard.

Chapter
TWELVE

"WE CAN'T COME TO THE PHONE RIGHT NOW because we're down at Sister's sorting eyeballs. Call us there if you need us." That's the message Babe left on her answering machine. If Daddy calls, I hope he gets worried. Maybe he'll take off and head down the highway. If he does, I hope he leaves Jewel with the dinosaur. She'll be all right.

This taxidermy lady has a lot of nerve. She ain't even met me before, and she's already wanting favors. I would say no, tell her I'm not helping match up no eyeballs or any other kind of body part. But I don't know Babe too well yet. She might get mad and send me to Jake's, and well, Jake is worse than taxidermy, I'm pretty sure.

I already told about all those dead animals staring out the windows. It's a brick house, painted blue, which is a waste of good brick if you ask me. I never heard of a blue house, and I hope I never have to see one again. It ain't right. Plus she got bottles hanging in the trees, Pepto-Bismol, Aunt Jemima's pancake syrup, bread-and-butter pickle bottles, nothing pretty or unusual, just bottles out of the grocery store. Babe says Sister don't like to waste nothing. I believe it. She don't even like to waste dead stuff. And she's got plenty of that.

Except in the garage. I figure she's got something one hundred percent alive and mean living in there. There's signs posted all over it. Do Not Enter! Danger! Beware! Stay Away If You Know What's Good for You!

"What kind of dog's in there?" I ask.

Babe says, "Get out of the car. I'll show you."

I'm not sure I want to meet no killer dog, but she laughs and says to come on. This dog hardly ever bites.

She parks the Mustang next to the garage door underneath the windows, which are way up high and narrow like eye slits. They're also covered so you can't see inside. "I've got a key," Babe says. "Don't tell Sister, but I'll give you a quick peek."

I stand way back. Babe fits the key into the lock and slides up the door a few inches.

I can't see nothing or hear no barks or growls.

"Come on, Matchit. You'll want to see this." She raises the door a couple of feet.

I bend down real slow and look. I can't see much except wheels.

It ain't nothing but a car.

She pushes up the door all the way. What I see makes me catch my breath. It's red. It's shiny, not one dent.

Perfect. This Sister woman's got a Corvette, a classic '66, one of the prettiest cars ever made. I never saw a car like this except in a magazine.

"This is Sister's pride and joy," Babe says. "She's so particular with it. Doesn't even want the dust from outside touching it. Of course, she has to drive it fairly often to keep it running, but it's mostly at night, and always on the highway. These country roads are deadly." Babe grins. "So what do you think of the mean dog?"

I like it. She promises I'll get to see it again, but for now, we got to go inside. We got work to do.

Sister is in the living room waiting for us. She don't look like a lady who would own a muscle car. She's tiny with big black glasses, a little pointy nose. Give her some long whiskers she might be a mouse. You think a taxidermy woman who cuts up dead animals would wear old bloody clothes and a mask like a doctor? You're wrong. This woman is all dressed up like she's going to a funeral.

"You must be Matthew," she says, bending her head and letting her glasses slip down on her nose. She looks over the rims at me.

Babe corrects her right up front. "His name is Matchit, Sister. I told you that."

"He sure is skinny." Sister looks me over, walking around in a slow circle, clicking her tongue at everything. "I see his ribs from here. Umph! He's got about four cowlicks, too. Why are the tops of his ears so red?"

Who does she think she is? The school nurse? Is she going to tell me to get on the scales and get weighed? This lady's making me jumpy. I shove my hands in my pockets and look down at the floor. Finally, she leaves me alone.

"Come see what I bought at the auction," she says. "I got a bargain this time." She goes into the other room and comes back with a mop bucket as big as the custodian uses at school. It's full of eyeballs, all sizes. They didn't cost her nothing, hardly. She says you're in luck if a taxidermist dies and the relatives don't know the value of their equipment. People don't know how expensive glass eyes can be, she says, how some of these things are painted by hand. Some are made in Germany.

The taxidermy lab is in the basement. We have to walk down the stairs in a single line because the steps are so narrow, Sister first, then Babe, then me. As we're going down the stairs, Sister's lecturing about how we're going to match up the eyes in pairs. "Every eyeball has to match its twin *perfectly*. And be careful," she says, "these eyes can be damaged. Do not grab them in your fists. Do not drop them on the cement floor. Do not squeeze them too hard. Do not scratch them with your fingernails."

How do you mess up a fake eye? This woman is crazy. Mean, too.

"As I said earlier," she continues, "some of these things are hand-painted from Europe. They're valuable. If you have a watch or rings on, take them off. I don't want any scratched irises." Babe don't say much, just uh-huh, uh-huh to everything. I guess she's used to being bossed.

What I think is this Sister lady sure puts a lot of stock in how something dead is supposed to look.

Down in the basement there's a big wooden workbench and all kinds of tools. She has hand drills hanging on the wall, big wrenches, hammers, and a lot of tools I can't name. Some, I bet, are for digging out the real eyeballs of animals so you can put the glass ones in.

Hanging from the ceiling is a big striped bass, two feet long, probably. That fish has eyes that are huge, black and shiny. It seems like they're following me.

Sister keeps looking at me, too, at my eyes. I bet she's thinking *What size spoon would I need to scoop out that boy's eyes?* That woman is spooky and weird. Some other things she is: bossy, plus nosey.

She hardly knows me and she's asking questions. What kind of grades you make? You like school? You like to read books? You been to a museum? You smart?

"Leave him alone, Sis," Babe says. "He's a fine boy. Real fine. Smart as a whip. Sharp as a tack. He's in Gifted and Talented, don't you know."

That woman can lie.

Sister cocks her head to the side. You can tell she don't believe it, but she's not gonna argue. She looks at me and squints her eyes like she's accusing me of cheating on a test.

"You ought to come be my apprentice. I could teach you the taxidermy trade. It'd give you something to do when you grow up. You already have plans on what you're going to be?"

I wish I could be a pilot. I'd take people wherever they want to go. I would have my own plane, and I'd fly kids for free, especially kids who don't want to get left nowhere. But you got to be a good student to fly a plane, at least AB honor roll. You got to have good eyes, which I do have that.

I always get a stomachache on career day. I will urp all over everything if anybody makes me go to school. I don't want nobody laughing at me. I don't want the teacher saying you want to be a pilot? You think a pilot has a 36 average in English? A 64 in mathematics? Boy, you'll be lucky to get a job folding napkins and filling up catsup bottles and salt shakers at Furr's Cafeteria.

I tell Sister no, I don't have no plans on what I'm going to be when I grow up.

"Why not?" she asks. That, I do not answer. This woman got no business asking me personal questions, snooping around, stepping on my insides.

"I think you could be a taxidermist," she says. "You have the hands for it. Let me see those fingers of yours."

I don't want her looking at my hands. I shove them in my pockets as quick as I can.

She turns back toward her workbench. It's got piles of tools everywhere, and the wood has got dark splotches all over. I think I know why.

"You know what this is?" she asks, waving around a pair of pliers.

I know they are long-nose pliers, and I say so. I ain't no fool. I do know tools.

She shakes her head so hard, I'm expecting something to fly across the room. "Not pliers. This is an ear opener," she says, looking as happy as pie that I was wrong. "See, when you squeeze, the jaws open instead of close. You might need one of these to help you spread open the ears if you're skinning something big." The whole time she talks to me, she is looking at my ears.

"You have to separate the cartilage from the skin. Same goes for the nose. It's not always that easy, either. Sometimes you have to soak the head for hours."

Babe's listening while she pairs up eyes. She's poured some in a box lid and she's rolling them around with her fingers, looking for two that go together.

"What color do you think a blue jay's eyes are, boy?" Sister asks.

"Blue?" I answer.

"They're black," she says. "What color are a canary's?"

"Black?"

"Brown. You wouldn't think a little yellow bird would have brown eyes, now would you? What color eyes does a chicken have?" Sister asks us both.

Babe says, "Hazel."

"Redtail hawk?"

"Red," Babe answers quick.

I feel like I'm stuck on an elevator with *Jeopardy!* These people know every dumb question and answer in the whole wide world.

Sister starts talking about how the Egyptians made their mummies. She says they pulled the brain out through the nose. I'm about to get a little interested when she picks up a tool from the workbench. "What do you suppose this is?" She holds up a wire thing that's curved like a spoon at the end.

I don't do nothing but shrug. I ain't guessing this time.

"This, my boy, is a brain spoon. You have to remove the brain, you know. This one's for small brains." I feel her eyes boring into the top of my head. "I use it on birds, mostly," she adds.

I got a brain bigger than a bird. She better quit looking at me.

Babe holds a pair of yellow eyes up to the light. "These for a bald eagle?"

Sister answers yes, but says she probably won't be doing no bald eagles. "Give them to Matthew," she says.

I don't especially want those eagle eyes, but Babe hands them to me, and I put them in my pocket.

"You know what a diorama is?" Sister never quits. What? You have to be dumber than a rock you don't know that.

Teachers love dioramas. You got to make one for just about every single thing you study. Here's how you do it: First you get a shoe box, then you paint the inside with black tempera or blue, whatever, then you glue in some stuff. It's like a display. Last year everybody had to do a diorama of a state motto. I picked Kansas because it's where my mama was born. I still remember the motto: *Ad astra per aspera,* which means, To the Stars Through Difficulty. It was easy making the diorama. I just painted the box black, hung a few stars from the top of the inside, sprinkled on some silver and gold glitter, and I was done.

I set it down on the floor next to the coffee table, and it looked pretty good until Jake came over. He was acting his usual stupid self, had his T-shirt pulled up playing like he was a belly dancer, and he accidentally planted his big fat foot on my sky.

Sister can't say enough about how taxidermists fix up those museum dioramas, how they bolt the animals' feet onto rocks and hills made out of papier-mâché and real dirt, and even fake pools of water. How people walk by, take pictures, pointing and talking about how natural everything looks. She says people love it when they can still enjoy something that's dead. It's a common fact that Roy Rogers had his horse Trigger done.

Sister is proud of her taxidermy animals, you can tell. To her, it's an art to make an animal look almost alive. Me, I'd rather see the thing while it's moving.

Sister must be able to see straight into my brain.

"You curious about whether I killed these animals myself?" she asks. She narrows her spooky eyes at me. "I used to hunt, but I don't do it anymore," she says. "Got rid of my guns. Now, people just bring me animals, fish mostly. Brother used to shoot birds, though, dove, quail, pheasant. Beautiful birds. We'd eat the meat, of course. You sure don't have much meat on your bones."

This lady makes me nervous.

"You have to be careful to use small shot, though, or you'll cause too much damage," Sister warns. "Brother would carry them by the feet so the feathers wouldn't get too ruffled, and let them cool down before he started the skinning. I used to wash off any blood that'd got in the way, then put 'em in the freezer. Fish, I wrap them in a wet towel, then put them in plastic bags until I get around to working on them. Want to look?"

I shake my head.

"Come here, Matthew," she says, moving toward the freezer.

"It's Matchit," Babe says, for the second time.

Sister stops in front of the freezer, which is a long white box, about three feet tall, about that wide, and maybe five feet long.

"What kind of name is Matchit?"

I shrug my shoulders like I always do when I don't feel like explaining.

She says my name sounds Egyptian. "Sounds like it'd be written on a mummy case inside a pyramid," she says. "You sure you're not dead?"

I feel the chill bumps crawling up my back and down my arms. This woman makes me cold and the freezer's not even open yet.

She reaches out and grabs hold of my elbow bone. She pulls me toward the freezer, then opens the latch and pushes up the lid. I can feel the frosty air hit me and I jump back. You scared to look, boy?

No, I ain't. I look inside.

This woman's got a whole zoo in there. I back up, squeezing my eyes shut, pressing my hands against my ears, trying not to hear what my brain is saying. You'd fit in that freezer real good, bad-luck boy. Wouldn't have to bend your legs or nothing. Ha!

Sister slams the door shut.

"My goodness, it's late," Babe says, looking at her watch. "Midnight. This boy's got to get to bed." She already broke a rule in the child-raising book. I yawn a couple of times. Make it clear how tired I am. I want out of here. And quick.

"Got your eagle eyes?" Sister asks as we head out the door.

I nod.

"What color eyes do you think a mockingbird has?"

I yawn again, and Babe says to leave me alone. "I think we've had enough about eyeballs for one night," she says.

I agree. I've had enough. I've got eyeballs on the brain.

Chapter THIRTEEN

IN MY BED ON THE PORCH, MY BRAIN KEEPS DOGGING ME. So, Matchstick, it whispers, bad-luck boy, how do you like this pretty place your daddy dumped you at? You got a crazy sculptor man, a fat little woman who can't quit talking and laughing, a taxidermy lady with a brain spoon, and a pile of junk big as a mountain. Ha!

I close my eyes and order my brain to go to sleep. It don't. It plays tricks on me all night long. All those dead animals come up out of the freezer. They float up to me with their frozen tongues sticking out, their empty eye sockets. They want their eyeballs. I try to run, but my feet have turned into blocks of ice. The cold rises to my knees, then up my elbows. My fingers are icicles. My eyes are cold, and when in my dream I look in the mirror, they are ice cubes. Even my scream comes out in a frozen lump. All the sudden I wake up. I'm sweating all over.

It's morning.

Babe is at the door with a breakfast tray. "Sister and I are going to an estate sale, and we have to leave early. If you want to go, you can."

"I'll stay," I tell her. Daddy's got to call. I been here long enough, three weeks almost.

"Would you mind watching the counter while I'm gone? Zebby will be here to look in on you, so you won't be here by yourself."

I frown at the part about Zebby. I don't need no baby-sitter.

She grins and says she knows how mature I am. She says I'm gifted and talented and very responsible. She won't be gone but a couple of hours, and she knows I will be just fine.

"If you get bored, there's some books under the counter," she says.

That's a big fat joke. I have to be more than bored to read a book. I'd rather eat a grasshopper.

She tells me she had polio when she was a kid. Her daddy read to her every single day, hoping she'd stay alive to hear the next page. "I never spent one day in an iron lung. I was one of the lucky ones," she says.

Does she think a book made her well? Sorry, books make me sick.

"One of those books is about a fisherman. Do you like to fish?"

Can that woman see into my brain? Of course I like

fishing. But I don't like books, even if they are about fishermen.

"It's about a man who catches a fish eighteen feet long."

Now, that sort of gets my attention. I could get interested in that kind of story if I could go right to the page about pulling in the fish. I wouldn't want to have to read a whole lot of pages just to get to the best part, though. So I tell Babe I'll be fine. I won't get bored.

When she leaves my room, I eat the breakfast she made, an egg-bacon-cheese sandwich and hot cocoa with marshmallows. I get dressed, brush my teeth, and walk into the front room to watch the counter. I sit down on the stool and pick up Babe's deck of cards. I know how to play solitaire, but I don't like it. It's boring. I do like to shuffle the cards, but even that gets old after a while. I like to draw, but I'm not in the mood. I figure until Daddy calls, it's going to be one slow day. There's not even a sound except for the ceiling fan. It makes a soft whir, and every few seconds there's a click. Whir . . . whir . . . one . . . two . . . three . . . click. Four . . . five . . . six . . . click. That thing needs some oil.

I wonder what kind of bait that fisherman was using. You'd have to use something big, a lot bigger than a worm or a minnow, or a shrimp. No kind of lure is going to work on a fish like that.

My brain interrupts my thoughts. What are you talking about, loser boy? Don't you know nothing? Nobody catches a fish that's eighteen feet long. How could one person reel it in, even if he did catch it?

One thing I do know. I'm not reading a whole book to find out, even if it's a skinny book, which it's probably not. Most books are fat. I look under the counter to prove it. Out of all of the books there, the one with the fisherman on the cover is the smallest. *The Old Man and the Sea*. It's only about as thick as my little finger, but I don't even like little books. And there's probably no pictures. So forget it.

I might look at the book if it had a picture of the fish, but I'm pretty sure it doesn't. Books with a lot of little bitty words don't have pictures. Just to be sure, I pull it out from under the counter and thumb through the pages. Nope. Not one picture. I slam it shut and put it down.

In my head the telephone rings. I pretend Daddy is on the line. I'm coming, Matchit. I stopped at Lucky's to use the phone. Get your stuff packed. Guess what? We're going to the Rocky Mountains for a little vacation, just you and me. We're going to sleep in a tent, go fishing for some speckled trout, camp out for a few days. Jewel? Forget her.

My insides get excited like it's really true, but I know it's not. Daddy's way up by Mount Rushmore.

The air from the fan lifts the edge of a plastic grocery bag on the counter. It flutters like it's about to take off, and it reminds me of how to make a parachute from a bag like that. First, cut the bag into a square. Babe's got scissors handy, so that's easy. Poke a hole in each corner. Tie four pieces of string about a foot long into each hole.

Babe's got lots of string. Tie the ends of the four strings together. Tie something onto that, something a little bit heavy, but not too heavy. A sinker might do, but Babe don't have no fishing gear in sight.

I look around. A spark plug is too heavy.

I'm looking all around the room, trying to think what might work.

I'm about to tie on a wing nut that's pretty lightweight when something thumps loud against the side of the house. Thump. Thump. I pick up a lug wrench and walk toward the front door.

I'm outside looking around when I hear Freebie, the stray that comes around looking for free stuff to eat. He's barking like crazy. I walk around the side of the house. He's gotten into it with some of Babe's pigeons.

"Get out of here," I holler. He takes off around the corner of the house. Then I look around at what he done. One bird is killed, anybody can tell that. His head is bent and he's got a mess coming out his belly. Another bird has a ripped throat, but he's still alive, squirming around like he's having a bad dream. My brain says Leave him alone, bad-luck boy. You can't do nothing. In five minutes, maybe less, he'll be dead.

I'm standing there holding the lug wrench, watching him, his wings beating the dirt, and I'm wondering if he's hurting real bad. "Hurry up and die, bird! You'll feel better." I tell him, but he won't lie still. What I want to know is why is he fighting so hard? Somebody tell him he's hanging on to the edge of the world, and if he don't try, he'll drop?

I ain't touching him. He'll be dead for sure. I look out across the yard toward Zebby's school bus. He's outside, bending down working on something. He ain't paying no attention to anything going on by the house.

It's just a stupid pigeon, but my stomach feels all knotted up inside. The best thing would be to put him out of his misery. This big heavy wrench would do it. I raise my arm. Nope. I can't. I set the wrench down. There's a pile of concrete blocks stacked next to the house. I pick up one with both hands and carry it over to the bird. I hold it over his head. It would only take a second, and I wouldn't even have to watch. All I'd have to do is close my eyes and let go. He wouldn't hurt no more. I squeeze my eyes shut and count: one . . . two . . . three. My fingers won't move.

Matchstick, you big baby. Drop it. But I can't let go. I set the block down on the ground.

My brain tells me to go back inside the house, pretend I never saw this bird. Let him die on his own. Getting hurt is what happens when you get in a fight with something bigger than you. Make him learn his lesson.

That bird looks at me with his little yellow eyes, and suddenly, I take off. I'm running through the yard, jumping over rusty pieces of cars, through weeds, in and out around the cars, all the way to Zebby's bus. He's sitting in a lawn chair taking apart a fan motor.

"I'm busy," he says.

"I know. But a dog got a hold of some of Babe's pigeons. One of them, I think, is still alive."

Zebby keeps working.

"I think he's hurting pretty bad."

He grumbles something under his breath and sets the motor down in the dirt. He gets up and follows me through the yard and when we get to the pigeons, he squats in the dirt. He scoops up the hurt bird and looks him over.

"It's just his craw." He pulls the feathers apart at its throat and shows me the mess of sticky seeds coming out the ripped part.

"Maybe we could take him to a vet?"

"Not around here."

"Is he going to die?"

Zebby sighs. "Wait here." He turns around and walks back out to his bus.

When he gets back, he's got a needle threaded with long black thread. In the other hand, he's got an empty cardboard box. He sets the box on the ground and picks up the pigeon.

"Hold him," he says.

My brain warns me straight up. Don't do it, Matchstick. You touch that thing, he'll die for sure.

"I might drop him."

"Here," he says, and he puts the bird into my hands.

He sews quick and sure, and after he ties the knot and cuts the thread, he puts the pigeon into the box and walks off.

I carry the box into the house and set it on the counter. The bird slides to the end of the box. He's a ball of feathers that's trembling all over, and I figure he's hurting like crazy.

"If I touch you again, it probably can't make things worse. You're already a goner." I touch him real light with the tip of my finger. His feathers are smooth and soft. When I run my finger down the edge of his wing, he don't even move.

I look over at the book sitting on the counter beside me. The fisherman on the cover is old and wrinkled. He don't look like he could catch a little bitty crappie, much less an eighteen-foot marlin. Babe thinks she stayed alive just to hear what would happen on the next page? That's the dumbest thing I ever heard.

"It's just your craw," I remind the bird. "It's not like you got your heart ripped or anything." I sit in the quiet and watch him. And I wonder how long it takes a bird to die.

"Okay, one sentence," I whisper. "It's not because I believe what Babe says." I want to make sure he understands that. I read the first line, and when I'm finished, I can't believe what I just read. That old man fished for eighty-four days straight without catching nothing. "This book is stupid," I tell that bird. "You got one crazy fisherman here. Sorry. I ain't reading no more. You're going to have to get well by yourself." The bird shivers and draws himself into a tighter ball.

"Okay. Two more sentences. No more," I tell him. I just want to see if the man catches the giant fish. If he does, that's all I'm going to read. The first sentence says a boy fished with the old fisherman for forty days, but his parents made him quit because they weren't catching anything. The next sentence is the one that tells the truth. It says the old man was unlucky. Now that I understand.

"This man is a lot like me," I tell the bird. His yellow eyes stare straight ahead. "I guess you're unlucky, too." I shut the book.

Not one feather on that bird moves. We both sit there all morning, me waiting on the phone, him waiting to die. Neither one happens. Daddy don't call, and when Babe gets home, that bird is still breathing.

The first thing when she walks in the door she wants to hear all about what happened. She wants details.

"Tell me the whole story," she says. "Now, what happened? Don't leave out a thing."

"It ain't nothing to tell," I answer.

It's the same thing I tell the testing ladies, the counselors, the assistant principal, and the teachers. Babe don't push it. "Well, okay," she says, real calm. "You don't have to tell me anything if you don't want to."

She pats me on the shoulder and says she'll be right back. In a few minutes she comes in carrying an old parakeet cage. It's got a little red bar swing and a mirror with a tiny brass bell hanging off the side. There's a little white plastic cup for water and one for food. This cage is too small for a pigeon, she's saying, but it'll do. He just needs a place to stay until his throat heals up.

This bird is going to die in this cage. That's all.

Babe puts newspaper in the bottom of the cage and sets the bird into the middle of it.

"I have a mind to find somebody to take some buckshot after that stray," she says.

I know she don't mean it. Freebie will get his bone, just like always.

Chapter FOURTEEN

THE NEXT MORNING THAT BIRD IS STILL BREATHING. My brain says Bad-luck boy, don't start hoping about nothing. If you do, you'll just get disappointed faster.

I ain't hoping nothing, especially since he won't even try to eat. Babe tells me to try bits of whole wheat bread, but he don't want it. I'm just going to read three more sentences to this dying pigeon. Three. That's all. I flip through the pages and start reading the first part my eyes land on. The old fisherman drinks a cup of shark liver oil. Does he think that's going to help him catch a fish? I doubt it. I'm wondering what shark liver oil tastes like when I look up to see if the bird is dead yet. He's not. "Keep living, bird, and I'll keep reading," I tell him.

Daddy wouldn't believe I'm sitting here reading to a pigeon. He'd say I lost my marbles, which makes me smile, just a little. I do miss him, no matter what. In my head I see him clear as day, standing at the bathroom sink slapping cold water on his face, trying to get woke up like he does every morning. I'm bringing him a cup of coffee, three heaping spoons of sugar, no milk. I set it down on the back of the toilet. Wait. It's not me. It's Jewel bringing the coffee.

And I'm not at home. I'm at the junkyard. I close the book and set it back under the counter.

Babe's rattling around in the kitchen cooking my breakfast just like she has done every morning since I've been here. Don't she know I can take care of myself? Nobody can make a grilled cheese sandwich like I can. Matchit's Grilled Cheese: Turn the stove burner on medium. Put butter on the outside of two slices of bread, put two pieces of American cheese in between, two squirts of mustard, two slices of dill pickle, one blob of peanut butter. Slap it into a hot skillet. Brown on both sides. I don't need nobody to play mama.

My brain says You got an attitude, slow boy. That woman's trying to help you. You don't appreciate nothing.

Shut up.

I'm walking down the hall, smelling the bacon sizzling in the skillet, feeling the heat of the kitchen drift toward me. It will be hot outside again, too, but for now the linoleum feels cool on my bare feet. I stop at a row of pictures lined up on the wall: First, there's Babe at the junkyard when she was a little girl. She's sitting behind the steering wheel of a 1948 Ford. Behind her is the junkyard, and there's even more cars than now. There's lots more pictures of different people standing in front of the junk-yard. One shows two people, a man and a woman, stand-ing at a sign that says Donate Metal to the War. There's rows and rows of pictures stretching all the way back in time to when the yard was new.

There's been a lot of people at this junkyard. And now there's me.

"Good morning!" It's Babe. She's calling me from down the hallway. I thought she was cooking breakfast, but she's not. That woman is dragging a sawhorse into the kitchen. What in tarnation she got in her head?

After the sawhorse, she hauls in all kinds of building supplies: two-by-fours, hammers, nails, sandpaper, an electric jigsaw, screwdrivers. She grins at me and says she got a big surprise.

"Come sit down, Matchit," she says. "I got your break-fast fixed a long time ago. It's been in the oven keeping warm." She hands me a plate of food. There's two fried eggs sunny side up and two slices of bacon, which she has placed above the eggs to look like eyebrows, a slice of ap-ple for the mouth, a biscuit for the nose. It's downright embarrassing. She think I'm a baby?

"After you eat your breakfast, we're going to build us something," she says. She lifts one of the two-by-fours she's carried into the kitchen and holds it up high. It bumps into the light fixture, but she don't care, she laughs.

"We are going to make us some stilts!"

That woman got to think I'm some kind of idgit, first

eat a baby clown breakfast, then go walking around on two big sticks high enough to skin your butt on a telephone pole. You can't tell her nothing, though. She got her mind made up.

"You sleep good?" she asks.

I nod.

"How's the pigeon?"

"No change," I answer.

"Well," she says. She don't know what to say for once.

That pigeon don't even move. You'd think he's a taxidermy bird. Except he ain't mounted on a piece of wood with a name label. Not yet anyway. You want to hope he gets well? Forget it. It's just a bird. There's millions of them in the world. You think it matters when one gets hurt?

After I eat, Babe hands me a square of sandpaper. "You know how to sand?" she asks.

I know how to change the oil in a car. I know how to replace belts, fix flats, put in a new air filter. Heck, I can even put in an alternator. I can sand a piece of wood if I want to.

"Matchit?"

I look up.

"Do it like this," she's telling me. "Rub the sandpaper all one direction. Don't go in swirlies."

She think she got all the answers? Seems to me it don't matter how you sand this old piece of wood. Ain't like we're making furniture for a king. These are just plain old stilts. Plain old won't do for Babe. She says these stilts have to be exceptional. No kid living with her can have anything but. The wood has to be extra sturdy, sanded so there won't be no splinters, and varnished to keep the rain and the bugs out. She's drawn up directions on a piece of notebook paper, and she's so excited, she's decided to build herself some, too.

"I always wanted me some stilts," she says. Then she giggles. This part gets on my nerves. She's a grown woman, got gray hair, but she thinks she's a kid. I'm surprised she don't have braces on her teeth.

"What about you, Matchit? You always want some of these?"

I shake my head. Sometimes I want things, but it's not stilts. Here's what I want: Never have to go to school. Never stay with stupid Jake. Never go to Skate Ranch again. Never have to see Jewel. Never think about my mama.

My brain butts in. You got a bunch of nevers, boy. You're scared to say you want something, aren't you? What about that bicycle?

I shake my head. I never want a bicycle again. I'm done with wanting one. It is too much trouble.

Babe is sanding and sanding in long sweeps. Every so often she slides her fingers down the wood, feeling how smooth it is. Can you believe a grown woman making stilts? Something ain't right about that. Her body parts are way past grown-up size. Her brain is not. It's child-size.

"Matchit, when I was a kid, they called me Bulldog." I must've frowned because she says, "It's true, sugar. Look at this face of mine." She stretches her lips into a smile and with all the folds of skin around them and down into her neck, I see what she means.

"Imagine having a face like a bulldog and being short and squatty, too. Ever seen a bulldog up on top of a pair of stilts, Matchit?"

Babe's got a laugh like a big painted-up ball that bounces and rolls everywhere. You don't think it's ever going to stop. My brain says She think life is going to stay this way? Everything so easy, you sit around making stilts on the kitchen floor? She don't know nothing.

Babe goes on to say Zebby ought to get him some stilts, everybody on this whole wide world ought to get stilts. She says, "You get up on these things, you see the whole earth spread out underneath you. A person can be in charge of things." That woman is humming "The Star-Spangled Banner" she's so happy.

She don't know beans. You get high up in the air, what you see is a yard full of junk, cars without no wheels, cars so old they ain't nothing but a pile of rust. You can't climb on a pair of stilts and go around thinking you don't live in the real world no more. And Zebby, he don't need stilts. He already thinks he don't live in the world with everybody else. You ever heard of somebody making art out of car crashes?

And you'd think he at least cares about that bird, being he sewed him up. Don't worry. He don't. Soon as he finished with that pigeon, he walked off, didn't even look back.

My brain says Remember when your daddy left, how you watched his truck get smaller and smaller as it went down the road. First it was two red dots, then one, then it went out completely, like a cigarette butt that got stomped on. Now he's been gone twice as long as he said he would be. You think he cares about you?

"Matchit?" Babe says. "Penny for your thoughts." That laugh of hers bounces up again, crashing into me.

My heart stiffens up like a cat that got rubbed the wrong way.

I'm out of here.

When I get to my van, I look up and the first thing I see is that thing Zebby's building out by the bus. He's changed it again. Today it's got a sharp pointed top that jabs into the sky. Yesterday it looked like something wilted. What's wrong with that guy? Can't he make up his mind about nothing?

I yank open the van door and set myself down into the driver's seat. Grab the gearshift, stomp the clutch and shove the gear into first, then pop the clutch, shift into second, clutch, third. Errrrrrr—clutch again. I'm grinding that gas pedal into the floorboard. Hard. I'm in fourth gear, speeding over a hundred miles an hour down the highway. I'm knocking down everything in my way.

My brain says Matchstick, you know you're just pretending. You're just a dumb kid who believes what people say, the promises they make.

I answer loud and clear. No, I don't. Something that ain't happened yet is nothing. It's layaway.

Mama puts everything on layaway. I was with her when she put a down payment on a dining table at Value-Mart. She picked out a set of dishes with little green four-leaf clovers decorating the plates, two sets of drinking glasses with gold rims, a lamp with a remote control switch, a set of towels thick enough and big enough to wrap around three people, and the last thing—a bicycle. It was black with silver racing stripes. I never did get that bike.

Daddy said don't worry. I'm gonna get you a bike, Match, and it won't be no sissy cheap bike, like that one your mama almost got you. I'm going to get you a mountain bike with eighteen gears. It's going to have real chrome and a leather seat.

I'm thinking, yeah, and when school starts up, you're going to be there for me when I get sick and the nurse calls and says to come get me. You won't make me stay on that school cot all day telling everybody that my daddy will be there any minute. And you're going to drive Jewel to Mount Rushmore and come right back home. Five days. That's it.

My brain says Matchstick, you dummy, you believe anything.

I'm stomping the gas. It's 120 miles an hour, 125. This van's going so fast, it's a blur. I can't even see ahead where I'm going. I'm squeezing that steering wheel like it's something about to choke.

I hear footsteps. They're too heavy to be rats. Not light enough for Babe. Nope, it's Zebby.

He knocks on the passenger door.

I look straight ahead, but I see him out the side of my eye. He don't have to knock. The windows are open. He's poking his beard inside, then his whole head.

He says, "Phone call." He gives the van door a pat and heads on out to his place. I watch him walk away, his hands stuffed down in his pockets.

I go inside the house and pick up the telephone receiver. It's Daddy.

"You were right, Matchit," he says.

"About what?" I want to know.

"The truck. The timing chain went."

I don't say nothing.

He's sorry, real sorry, but he might not be able to make it for my birthday next week. He'll sure try, though. If he can't come, he'll call.

That part is a promise.

Chapter
FIFTEEN

YOU BETTER HURRY UP AND DIE, BIRD. I'm getting tired of messing with you. I've read too much of this fisherman book already, the first sentence on a whole lot of pages. I even read the part about catching the giant fish. I've read about the old man fighting sharks, about how he eats raw shrimp, eyeballs, tails, and all, and about his hands bleeding. It's took a lot of reading. And I hate reading.

You, bird, still won't get well.

I've piled up all the feathers you've lost. I've lined up untouched seeds all across the edge of the inside of your cage. You ain't even looked up. "You are dying one slow death," I tell him. "Don't you want to know if the old man is going to bring that giant fish in to shore and be a hero like he always planned?"

I lie on my bed out on the porch, wondering when that bird is going to give up. I hear Zebby hammering metal across the yard. He's changing his sculpture again. Clank clank clank. It goes on and on, pounding on my nerves, waking up my brain until it thinks it's going to scream. I put my hands over my ears. He's got a screw loose. That's what Daddy would say.

People who have a screw loose are crazy. Sometimes they're killers. I'm lying in bed cooking up a great story about Zebby. It's really scary, so scary I have to turn on the light. I take out my drawing tablet and sketch a killer Zebby climbing out the window of his bus. He looks a lot like Dracula. His teeth are dripping blood and he's wearing a black cape. His sculpture stands behind him, reaching up into the air like a gigantic spike. It reaches all the way to the top of the page. It pokes a hole in the moon.

My brain starts to laugh. You think these pictures are any good? Don't show them to nobody. You'll get laughed off the face of the earth.

I turn out the light, but my brain won't go to sleep.

What if Zebby can't figure out what he's building because he ain't no real artist? What if he's really some kind of secret killer? What if he decided to sneak up through the yard to my screened-in porch? The door has a latch, but all he'd have to do is use wire cutters to cut a hole in the screen, reach around, and open the door. I'd be sound asleep, but when he got next to my bed, I'd feel him standing there. I'd open my eyes, and what would I see? Dracula teeth.

I sit up in bed and look out over the yard. Zebby's light is on in his bus. He's not hammering anymore, and I figure he's gone inside for the night.

If he is a murderer, I wonder what he is doing.

When I wake up, it's the dead still part of the night. Except for one thing. I hear something far in the distance.

At first I'm pretty sure it's the television in Babe's room, but after a while I can tell it's not coming from inside the house. It's outside. The music is faint, but I got good ears, and when I look through the screen out over the dark yard, I see that the light is still on in Zebby's bus. The music is floating from that direction in a soft thin stream. It sounds a lot like something I've heard before, something my mama used to sing.

I get up, put on my jeans and my shoes. I don't need a shirt, but I do need a flashlight.

Matchstick? You crazy? You're shaking inside. You're going out there?

Yes, I say. I'm going to prove I ain't scared. I'm going to sneak over to the bus and peek into the window because I wonder what he's up to. And I wonder if murderers really listen to music like that.

I tiptoe down the hall to the kitchen. In the pantry on the third shelf between a case of motor oil and a case of creamed corn there's a flashlight. I borrow that, and when I see the long screwdriver lying next to it, I decide I need to borrow it, too. For protection. I put the screwdriver in my back pocket, but it falls out and hits the floor with a loud bonk.

Freeze, Matchit.

I hold my breath, waiting to see if Babe comes in to see

100

what's going on. She doesn't. I stoop down and pick up the screwdriver. I stick it through my belt loop like a sword.

It's not easy walking through a car junkyard in the middle of the night, even with a flashlight. You have to watch out for the rats and snakes, watch out for things that are jagged. I pretend I'm a sea diver, swimming through a dark and deep part of the ocean. Anything might swim up and grab hold of my pants, bite me on the leg, even.

The moon is shining just enough to make everything weird and watery. Some of the cars got their hoods crunched open. Their big glass eyes watch every move I make. Their mouths are sharp and jagged, and I can see some of the stuff they've swallowed sticking up out of their teeth like squirmy black intestines.

Suddenly my heart stands straight up like it got called to attention, and my brain is hollering at me. Matchstick, you big baby. You'd be scared of your own shadow. Those cars aren't sharks.

I feel like running, but I can't. Anyone knows you got to walk slow through a junkyard at night. When I'm almost at the bus, the music starts up again, the same song. I recognize a few of the words, even if I don't know what they mean. *See on the portals He's waiting and watching* . . . I'm not sure who's been waiting, who's been watching, but tonight it might be Zebby. And I feel even more scared.

His windows are open. The music is drifting out of them real easy like curtains blowing in a breeze. I scoot up closer. The notes are soft as baby feet. They make me feel like I want something real bad, but I don't know what.

I sneak up closer and turn off my flashlight. I squat down and think about what to do next.

After a minute, I creep toward the bus. A broken part of Zebby's sculpture is lying ahead of me, like some kind of huge bony thing with sharp edges stuck together every which way. When I crawl by, its sharp teeth rake into my ankle. I feel a warm bloody worm crawl across the hurt part.

My ankle stings, but I can't keep my eyes off what he's been building. Mixed in with the wrinkled-up doors and bumpers, there's razor-knife edges of steel and deep places of crashed metal. I feel it start to move, to swim toward me, and I feel my hand curl around the screwdriver tucked into my belt loop. One clap of those jaws might pull me along through the dark.

Matchstick? You going to cry for your mama, your daddy?

Shut up. I ain't crying for nobody. This thing is only a bunch of sawed-up metal, I tell myself, not a shark, not a monster, not anything, and the calm cool Matchit comes back.

I tiptoe to the edge of the bus, trying to figure out which window to peek in so Zebby won't see me. Holding my breath, I press my body against the emergency exit door and listen. I hear him walking in those clompy boots of his. He opens a drawer or something, then I hear a sound like Jake makes when he's sharpening his knife on a whetstone.

My mouth has gone dry and my hands feel cold. I hear

Zebby walk toward the front of the bus. Then the soft swoosh of his body sitting down in a chair.

I step onto part of Zebby's metal sculpture, putting my foot between two ribs, and stretch myself higher on my toes and look. I see the legs of a table. Then I see Zebby. He don't have no knife, just a piece of sandpaper. Something made of plaster sits on the table in front of him. He's also got a cup of pencils and some drawing tablets. He's got wadded-up paper everywhere. Zebby's head is down, but he's not drawing.

His face is pressed onto his arms and his shoulders are shaking. One thing I know. Killers don't cry.

He shifts his weight in the chair.

I pop down.

Even after the music stops, I'm waiting and listening.

I don't hear no moving around. I stretch up to the window and look again. Zebby is sitting up now, his chin in his hands.

I'm balancing on my toes, craning my neck trying to see. Then I slip.

Zebby turns, and I swing my whole body under the bus. At the same time I hear him walking, clunk clunk clunk in those heavy shoes of his. I hold my breath. Pretty soon he is at the door, opening it and walking outside. My heart climbs up into my throat like a big scaredy-cat. I crawl under the bus a little farther until I get a mouth full of sticky spiderweb. My ankle is hurting like crazy, and I got dirt in my eyes. And I smell oil and rust. Also I'm remembering. Snakes probably live under old buses.

I hear him climbing up his scaffold, and from under the bus I can see him.

He's standing way up high looking all around.

It's a long time after he's gone before I can crawl out from under the bus and run back to the house.

In my room, it's dead quiet. "You alive?" I whisper at the birdcage.

Nothing moves. "Hey!" I shout. Still no sound. That bird is dead, I'm pretty sure.

I crawl into bed. The next thing I know I'm waking up.

It's raining. I look around the room, letting my eyes adjust to the dark. The tarps are pulled down over the screens. So that's why the rain sounds like it's got cotton in its mouth. Babe must've snuck in while I was asleep, after I got back from Zebby's. She must have pulled down the tarps to keep the storm out.

I lean back onto the pillow. My head makes a picture and I let it drift around me quiet as smoke. I am in that tent in the mountains. My daddy is in his sleeping bag next to me. His breaths go in and out, soft and smooth. The night is cold and I scoot my bag close next to his. Pretty soon I feel his arm around me, hugging me close to him.

Outside is the trout stream where we'll fish the next morning, and as far as you can see, there's pine trees, like a million birthday candles stuck on the world. If you lie down under them, they're so tall you can't even see their tops, and you figure they've been growing on this earth for a thousand years before you was even born, and you feel so good here in the mountains with your daddy next to you.

The rain is coming down heavy, pounding on the cars outside, filling all the hard dry cracks in the ground. I smell it mixed with old metal and rust and dirt. Even with the tarps, some of it is coming through the porch screen, dripping along the edge of the floor. That pigeon still don't wake up, and I know I ain't on no campout. Daddy is a long ways off with Jewel. And another thing. I never slept under no pine tree.

The last thing I hear before I go to sleep again is the drip drip drip of leftover rain coming off the roof.

Come morning, a thin edge of light sneaks from around the tarps and outlines the room. I stand up at the side of the bed and pull on my blue jeans. They slide down under my belly button, almost slide down past my hips.

Remember Jake teasing you about being so skinny? Remember how he said you're going to be a grown-up man with little boy parts? You got a winkie looks like it got squashed by a tractor?

"You're full of bull," I answer loud as I can, but my brain knows I don't mean it because I feel embarrassed of myself, my skinny body. I sit down and squeeze my legs together, pull them up to my chest, hold my arms close. You scared, Matchstick? Nobody's here. Nobody but you and a dead pigeon, probably.

I get up and pull the edge of the tarp away from the screen so that a piece of light shines into the room.

Wait. I hear something.

Shhhhhh. Listen.

"Your ribs stick out, boy. Don't you eat, boy, boy, boy?"

Who is that? Jake?

Boy, boy, boy, he coos.

"Shut up!" I say.

"Coo—coo—coo."

It's that bird. He ain't dead.

That bird is alive!

Chapter SIXTEEN

"WHOOPEE!" BABE HOLLERS. She raises her hands in the air, dances around in a circle. Next thing you know, she grabs hold of me and twirls around the kitchen. What's **this** woman doing? Finally, she lets go and two-steps right out of the room. She's going to go see that bird for her own self.

I don't think a person should get that caught up. It's only a pigeon. Don't she know that bird could keel over any minute? Who knows why he was hopping around? Could be he couldn't breathe good. I've seen people who couldn't breathe on *Real-Life Stories* on television. They squirm like crazy before they die. Some probably hop around, too.

She comes back in with the cage swinging from one arm. "You should name this fellow Lucky," she says to me.

"He's already got a name. Dog."

"Dog," she says, letting the word roll around in her mouth. "Dog," she says again. "Well now, that's a good name, a strong name. It's something to live up to. I do like that name."

"Howdy do, Dog," she baby-talks into the cage wires. "You going to be as brave as your name?" She tells that pigeon all about the sunflower seeds he's going to get for getting well, how crunchy and good they'll taste, how she's going to take his picture, how he's a miracle bird since he lived after getting his throat ripped, then sewed up. She goes on and on. That woman, she'd talk to a Cheerios box if you gave her a chance. Finally, she sets the cage on top of the refrigerator. "A bird belongs high up, even if he is in a cage," she announces.

She faces me and smiles like I won something, then she reaches out to hug me. I cross my arms in front of my chest.

She steps back and says, "Maybe we should go out and tell Zebby about the bird?"

"He's not worried."

Babe says it's true, a great artist doesn't have the mental energy to worry about pigeons. She says it's okay, though. She'll be happy to do everybody's worrying for free. She's got a lot of space in her brain, especially for people she loves.

"Sit down here at the table," she says to me. "Let me do some of your worrying, Matchit. What do you want me to take on for you?"

These are the things I don't tell her: First, is my daddy.

What if he don't make it back at all? What if Jewel changes her mind and decides she likes him after all? What if I have to stay with Jake the Jerk? Then school. It's a permanent aggravation. After that, my mother.

"So you got any worries, honey?" Babe asks again.

"Huh?" I look up. "I ain't worried about nothing."

She says that's good because she's got an idea she wants me to hear.

"I've been thinking," she says. "I don't have children of my own, so I don't have any grandchildren. I don't even have a niece or a nephew. Matchit, maybe you could unofficially adopt me. I could come to your school on award days, things like that."

She think I'm going to get an award? I might. The kid who lost his homework the most days in a row. Skinniest boy who got the biggest teeth that stick out the most. The boy who had the most fights in one school year.

"I've been thinking about something else, too. Do you have a college fund?"

"A what?"

"A savings account to pay for your future education. I calculate it's going to take at least twenty thousand dollars a year, and that's just for a state school. There's dormitory fees, meal tickets, books. College takes four or five years, at least. I don't have the money yet, but I'm getting some ideas."

Babe says that Sister goes to auctions all over the county. This time she had the chance to make a good investment on fishing boats. She bid on twenty-seven worn-out boats at an auction over in Shreveport, and she won the bid. Babe says Sister loves to bid on stuff. She'll bid on a box of water pipes if they're cheap enough, and the boats were cheap as dirt.

"It's our first investment for the Matchit McCarty Scholarship Fund," Babe says. "We can fix up the boats and sell them. They won't pay your whole way to college, but it'll be a start."

I shove both of my hands in my pockets. My brain asks me two questions. You need college to teach you how to fry hamburger patties at Burger Boy? You think you got to take French class to sell French fries?

College is not for me.

You can't tell Babe that, though. She's all fired up to get started. She says that when the boats arrive, somebody's got to figure out which ones might float, which ones might not, what parts we can remove to sell, what is useless, what is not.

"You know anything about boats, Matchit?"

"I know a little." I don't tell her I never been in a boat in my life.

That night I read Dog a few more lines from the fisherman book. I flip through the pages, reading a sentence here and there. It seems like those sharks aren't ever going to quit.

Finally, I put the book down and draw a picture. The fisherman is standing in the boat holding a club. His hands are dripping blood. He thinks he's going to beat away all those sharks with one stick?

"See this?" I say to Dog, showing him my drawing. "That fisherman don't got a chance."

It's six o'clock the next morning and barely light out when Babe knocks on my door.

"Matchit, the boats are here."

How can you have twenty-seven boats show up in the middle of the night? I didn't hear a thing. Babe says she didn't either. "Ever since you came here, Matchit, it's been nothing but miracles. That pigeon getting healed, now this. You are Matchit the Miracle Boy."

I look out the porch screens over the yard. Sure enough, there are boats. They are stacked everywhere, in between the cars, on top of cars, even. These are not bright shiny fiberglass bass boats with outboard motors, trolling motors, and depth finders. They are not ski boats with padded seats, racing stripes, inboards and outboards. These boats are mostly old aluminum fishing boats. They got leaks around the rivets and holes punched in the bottoms and sides. They got dragged up out of rivers, probably. You could sell every single one of these things, and you wouldn't have the money to pay for a scholarship to the city jail. No wonder the owners unloaded them without making noise. They didn't want Babe waking up to tell them to forget it. These boats should be carted to the trash dump. Wait. They're already in a dump.

You sure can't tell Babe that. By seven in the morning she's already painting a sign: We Now Have Boats! It's the biggest joke in the world if you ask me, well, almost the biggest. Me going to college is the biggest.

111

I wonder when it was I got dumb. I was smart in kindergarten and first grade. Kindergarten, I knew all the steps to change a tire. I knew where the jack is in the car trunk, exactly where you have to position it underneath the car, how to jack up the car, use a lug wrench to take off the lug nuts. I told the whole thing at show-and-tell. My teacher said I was a genius.

First grade, I was still pretty smart. I took my own tool-box to school and showed what a crescent wrench is, a claw hammer, channel locks, a Stilson wrench, pipe wrench, and five kinds of screwdrivers. I've been handing tools to my daddy since I could crawl nearly. My teacher called me the tool boy. When I got to the next grade, the smart started wearing off. My brain's been telling me how dumb I am every day since.

It's especially telling me that today. You going to build what? it says when I'm outside rolling old tires up to my van.

I'm going to build me a tunnel.

What do you need a tunnel for? My brain's acting like it's my daddy.

I don't want to have to explain that I need a tunnel to crawl through. I need it to hide in to get away from all these boats that make fun of me about their stupid college fund. I need it to take me straight from my porch bedroom right to my van door. One thing we got a lot of around here is tires. Babe says I can use all I want. If you want to build a tunnel, you got to have two long rows of tires in stacks of three. You got to put the rows close enough together to support the tires on top. Those make the roof. You got to have a lot of tires to make a tunnel from the back porch to the middle of the yard. It takes all morning, past lunch and most of the afternoon. I don't even stop for lunch. Babe don't mind. She's gone to town to photocopy a hundred Boats for Sale signs.

"Nice tunnel," she says that night when I finally come in to eat supper.

I nod. My hands are full of blisters. My back and shoulders, my arms and wrists, my legs ache. I don't care. I got a pretty nice tunnel.

"You are an amazing kid," Babe says.

The next day I'm in the van thinking about how to fix it up better when Babe comes knocking on the front windshield. "Come out," she says. "I want to show you something."

I could crawl through the tunnel and disappear, but she looks excited. I open the passenger door and climb out.

"You know the houseboat?" Babe asks.

She points at the biggest boat on the lot. It's about twenty-five feet long with what's left of a cabin. You could walk inside it if there wasn't so much rotted wood. The paint is peeled off everywhere, and the wooden deck is full of holes.

She wants me to follow her out there to look at it. When we get there, I watch her climb up on the deck and holler across the yard toward Zebby's bus.

"Zebedee!"

We both look out toward his bus, but he ain't around.

Suddenly, Zebby pops up from behind the old Thunderbird on the west end of the lot way on the other end from the bus.

Babe waves for him to come on up. He's holding a crankshaft. Those things can weigh over fifty pounds, but he carries it easy.

He makes his way real slow across the yard, carrying that greasy old crankshaft.

"I just got an idea," Babe says. "I'd like both of you to hear about it. It's about Matchit's scholarship fund."

Zebby frowns. He's probably thinking I walked all the way over here for this?

Babe says, "We could make this houseboat into a Chapel of Love to raise money."

He drops that heavy crankshaft down in the dirt. Babe has just gone and flipped her lid.

She starts listing plans. "Zebedee, you and Matchit could paint this boat white. We could set out some sweetheart roses. White or pink? What do you two think?"

We ain't thinking nothing. We don't know what this woman is talking about.

"Don't you know what a Chapel of Love is?"

Zebby's standing there with his hands in his pockets like he don't know nothing.

"A Chapel of Love is a place for people to get married. Without any fuss," she adds.

I peek out the corner of my eye at Zebby. He ain't believing what he's hearing. His eyes have gone hard like dried-up peas.

Babe keeps on talking. Zebedee could be a best man, she's saying. Matchit, you could be an usher. The couples wouldn't have to worry about a thing. They could say their vows, have some punch and cake, then go on about their business. For a fee, of course. We could have different rates. There'd be the deluxe wedding package, top of the line on that one. That would include mints, cashew nuts, those little egg sandwiches with the crust peeled off, pink punch with sherbet floating on top. After that could be the average plan, leave off the sandwiches and the sherbet on that one. Do you think we need a thrift plan? Folks avoid thrift when it comes to marrying, she tells us.

Zebby don't like it. You think he's going to dress up in a suit? He listens as long as he can, then he picks up his crankshaft and heads on out.

Babe talked nonstop about that Chapel of Love for two days, then she finally let go. It was already costing too much and it wasn't even out of her brain yet. First, you'd have to hire a preacher, then there'd be all the fix-up costs of paint, music, artificial flowers, and a whole lot of other things to make something decent. She said she didn't know why she even concocted such a dumb idea.

What I think is this: Babe could see her own self in a fancy white dress walking down the aisle of the fixed-up houseboat. She could hear that big organ music that sounds like giant bones getting dug up, and she could picture me in a suit and Zebby, too, waiting up front with the groom. I think she knew it couldn't happen. Not just the money it'd cost to put it on and not just all the hard work. She got stuck on one part. The groom. She couldn't fill in the blank.

The Chapel of Love was one dumb idea. When I tell him about it, Dog agrees. He bobs his head and scratches on the newspaper at the bottom of his cage. I read a little more of the fisherman book to him. The sharks keep taking bites out of the fish, and the old man's still fighting.

Dog's bored. Even a pigeon knows when it's time to give up. I put the book down and slide my finger through the cage and touch him. I tell him all about the tunnel, how good a place it is. "You want to see it, boy?"

My brain butts in. Hey, Matchstick, you think a pigeon is going to answer you? You told that bird all about the fisherman story, Babe's boats, the scholarship fund, the Chapel of Love, even that tunnel. That bird might eat from your finger, nod his head like he understands everything you tell him. He don't. He ain't even listening.

Matchstick, you so lonesome you got nothing better to do than talk to a pigeon?

Chapter SEVENTEEN

ONE WEEK AFTER THE BOATS CAME, BABE GOT LUCKY. A trucker passing through town saw one of the boat ads in the grocery store window. He knew someone in Oklahoma who was looking for some boats. The next day Babe had an order for twelve recycled aluminum fishing boats, one hundred dollars each. Now there's work to do. The holes got to be welded, the wooden seats sanded and painted. Those boats got to be safe and they have to look good.

We're all outside. Babe, Zebby, and me. She's talking, talking, talking, explaining everything. The boat seats have to be painted bright colors, red, blue, yellow, green, and there's plenty of each color, especially red because she got a bargain on that one. I don't think these boats will look sportsmanlike at all, but Babe says that's the point. These boats got sold to an amusement park in a little town in Oklahoma. They'll be used on a kiddie fishing pond.

"I need some help," she says to both of us. "I know you're busy with your sculpture," she says to Zebby, "but do you think you can do some welding for me?"

He puts his hands into his pockets and stares at his boot tops. "Might as well," he answers. I know the sound in his voice. I've heard it a million times. The teacher says, *Matchit, are you going to take a zero on this project?* I say, "Might as well."

He might as well work on boats. His sculpture ain't going nowhere. Every morning it's something different and every night it's different again. He can't figure out what it is, and I can't, either.

I do know a little bit about welding, but I never got to watch up close. So when he's ready to start, I'm walking up behind him. He's about to turn on the welder, but he takes off his helmet instead. He turns around and looks straight at me.

"You better go inside the house," he says.

"Can I watch?"

"It'll burn your eyes."

"I'll stand way back."

"No," he says.

I'm disappointed. I really do want to see him weld on those patches.

"I'll be careful. I've soldered before. I didn't get hurt."

He sighs and mutters something under his breath. "Wait here," he says. He walks out to his bus and comes

118

back with another welding helmet and an extra pair of gloves.

"If you're going to watch, you have to wear this helmet. Looking at a welding torch is like looking at the sun, you won't even realize the damage until it's too late. You want scars on your eyes?"

I never heard Zebby talk so much. He hands me a helmet that's too big, but it will do. He also hands me some leather gloves that reach all the way past my elbows. They're way too big, too, but I don't care. The helmet is heavy, but it feels good. It smells like the monkey bars at school, a mix of metal and sweat. The goggles are green plastic, scratched and kind of foggy. But they're okay.

"Stand back," he says, while he puts his helmet back on. "The torch is unruly. If you're not careful, it can fly out of your hands." He unrolls his sleeve and shows me a scar, flat and rough like a shingle on a roof. "This is why you have to hold on tight to the torch. You have to use both hands."

"It's like the water hose at the car wash," I tell him. "You let go and you got water spraying all over the place."

"This is dangerous." Zebby frowns at me. He don't want me fooling around. Or joking.

He bends down to turn on the welder. The torch shoots to life, and the sparks fly. He turns the rod to the metal patch he's attached to the side of the boat and melts a silver river around the edges. The helmet gets heavier and warm against my cheeks, but I don't care. I like what I see. I could weld. I know I could.

Zebby welds three patches onto the aluminum. He's ready to start on another boat, but before he does, he turns off the torch.

"You want to try?"

What? I can't believe it.

"You mean weld?"

"You have to let me stand behind you and help you hold the rod. You have to be careful and steady," he warns.

Yes! I'm going to weld!

"I'll be careful."

I'm not worried. I just want to weld.

Zebby motions for me to stand in front of him. He puts his arms around me and helps me hold the torch.

"Ready?" he asks.

I nod. With one of his hands holding my hands together and the torch, he reaches with the other hand to turn on the welder. It makes a roar and the tip lights up like a sparkler. Suddenly, it's come alive in my hand. I'm a knight holding my sword. Wait. I'm Luke Skywalker.

This sword glows red, and with Zebby's hands wrapped around mine, I hold it smooth and steady. The hot rod melts the patch onto the aluminum and seals the hole in the bottom of the boat. This boat will float for a few more years.

When it's time for a break, we sit on the bench seat inside the boat.

"You've done this before," Zebby says.

"No." I shake my head. "This is my first time."

"Sure?"

"Yes. I'm sure. I never welded before."

"You did a good job."

"Is that all there is to welding?"

"That's about it," he says, rubbing his hands together. "Not everyone is good, especially not at first."

It feels great to melt something so strong, to bend it and shape it, to make it obey you, do whatever you want it to do.

I don't get it. Why can't he finish his sculpture? Welding ain't that hard.

Every morning we get to work, welding, sanding, painting, everything. We're making pretty good time except for one thing.

Sister. She stops by at least once a day. Zebby and me, we both dread seeing her pull up.

She marches around, watching every move we make, acting like she's the big boss. "Be sure to use a tack cloth before you paint. Don't let the paint make drips on the seats. Be careful about getting those paint lids on tight. Clean those brushes good." She says we better do a good job. She didn't bid on those boats for nothing.

"You want to help paint?" Zebby asks.

She says no. She paints the fish she mounts, artistic things like that. She don't paint boat seats.

We're glad when it's time for her to go. Still, we make pretty good progress. And even though these

121

boats are old, real old, and not one bit fancy, I bet they will float.

"Babe says these boats are going to be famous," I tell Zebby.

He grumbles. "On a kiddie pond in an amusement park?"

"They'll be famous to the fish," I say.

He don't think it's funny.

Later he catches me looking toward his bus, looking at his metal sculpture. Every time I look at that thing, I wonder what it is. Is it some kind of monster? A scary mountain?

"Ever seen a piece of junk that big?" he asks.

"No," I say. "But I saw a fish that big."

Zebby raises his eyebrows.

"It was in the ocean." And then I add, "I caught it."

"Must've been quite a fishing trip."

My head is nodding like it don't even know it's lying, and once my mouth gets started, it don't know when to stop. "It was a marlin. Eighteen feet long. Over a thousand pounds. Took eighty-four days to catch it. The sharks tried to get it, but they didn't."

Zebby don't say nothing. I'm staring at the floor of the boat, but I feel him looking at me.

"You have it mounted?" he asks. "Is it at your house?"

My face is hot. I shake my head. Nope. In my head I just caught the fish. That was enough.

"Well," Zebby says. He sets down the tool he's got in his

hand. He just stands there quiet. It's so quiet I can hear flies buzzing across the yard.

"Well," he says again. *The Old Man and the Sea*. That's not an easy book for a kid."

My face is burning, my neck, too. I'm waiting on him to tell me to get out of here, to stay gone forever. To beat it.

He don't. He just got one question. "Did you read the whole book?" He don't seem to care I just told the biggest fish lie ever.

"Not all of it. Some of it's boring." I read about how the fisherman eats turtle eggs and raw shrimp, how he hurt his hands trying to fight off the sharks, but it takes about a million little tiny words for the fisherman to get back to the shore. I quit before that.

"You must not have read how the old man winds up with nothing but a fish head on the end of a skeleton. All that work. And time. For nothing." He takes a deep breath. "It's the irony of life."

"But he caught it." That's the important part.

Zebby don't care. He's finished. He picks up his helmet, his welding tools, all his stuff, and walks off.

Later, when Babe comes out, she's so happy about the boats, she brings me a fishing rod with a spinner bait and tells me to try a cast. She sets up an empty box on the hood of a junk car. "Stand in one of the boats and cast from there. Aim for the box," she says. "When you get good at that, we'll get you a coffee can."

It's not that easy to hit, but sometimes I do, and after a

while, I'm hitting that box every time just about. Pop! Set the hook. I got me one!

Babe says when it comes to pigeons and boats, me and Zebby, we're good. She says we done a miracle job. Those boats are fine, she says. And she ought to know. She buys a lot of junk.

Chapter EIGHTEEN

MATCHIT ARNOLD McCARTY, YOU FORGET YOUR BIRTHDAY?

No, I didn't. No kid forgets about a birthday. I just ain't talked about it. You talk about something, you start counting on it.

But Babe, somehow she found out. When I wake up on the morning of my birthday, there's streamers and balloons all over the place. Even the bathtub is full of balloons. I don't know what to do. But I can't help myself. I feel a little bit excited.

"Matchit?" Babe hears me come into the kitchen. She's halfway smiling, halfway biting at her thumbnail. There's something she ain't telling and finally, she can't stand it. "Okay," she says. "I could give you one little hint about your birthday." Her eyes are waiting for me to say something, but I don't. I'm scared to think.

"You have a surprise coming today."

My heart skips a beat. I ain't hoping for much. I just hope it drives up in a faded red 1983 Dodge pickup truck. And I hope it comes all by itself.

You're crazy, bad-luck boy. The surprise is probably just these cheap baby balloons. Let me tell you something. Your daddy's not going to get into that broken-down old truck of his, leave his precious Jewel, and drive all the way down here. Forget it.

My brain is a monster in my head. It gobbles up every good thought that comes along.

Still, all morning, I got a prickly feeling inside my skin. I'm excited and scared at the same time. If Daddy does show up today, on my birthday, I won't care if he brings a present or not. I might not even care if he brings Jewel. I'll just be happy that he came.

Babe says she's got some work for me. It'll help the time pass faster. She's written down three jobs for me to do (1) Answer the telephone (Daddy might call); (2) Go outside and holler at her when the buzzer on the oven goes off (It's supposed to go off every twenty-seven minutes); and (3) Wash a box of license plates (She's going to pay me five cents a plate).

She says she'll be outside, doing chores and some other things. But when I look out the window, she's tying a bed pillow around her rear with a rope. Next, she straps a bicycle helmet on her head. Anybody can figure out what she's going to do. If you see a short chubby woman walking on a pair of stilts, that's her. I guarantee it. Nobody else would be that crazy, not even my mama.

Every time the buzzer goes off, she will climb down from her stilts and come back inside to put four more cakes in the oven. Who told her my birthday was coming? Somehow she learned and she got twelve cake mix boxes sitting on the kitchen counter to prove it. She bought every kind of cake mix the store had: Devil's Food, Caramel Swirl, Strawberry Sprinkle, Vanilla with Cherry Bits, Chocolate Marshmallow, Fudge Royal, Butterscotch Supreme, Red Velvet, Pistachio Mint, and more, all different. After she stacks up the layers and puts on the icing, it will be the tallest rocket ship birthday cake anybody ever saw. You think I like rocket ships? I don't.

"How did you know it was my birthday?" I ask her.

"A little birdie told me," she says.

I know it ain't Dog. He can't talk.

It was Daddy, I bet. He called her up and said he wouldn't miss his kid's birthday for the world.

I'm sitting on the kitchen floor with the dirty license plates and a bucket of soapy water when the phone rings. I wipe my soapy hands on my jeans and run across the room to the telephone. I pick it up, say hello, and the voice at the other end says, "That sewed-up pigeon dead yet? You need me to come down and get him?" It's Sister, of course.

"He's just fine," I say. I bet she already had her brain spoon in her hand, ready to go.

Call number two: Somebody wants to know if we got a starter for a '94 Honda. We don't got nothing that new. But we do got boats, I tell them. No thank you.

Call number three: Wrong number.

I'll be lucky if I make fifteen cents the way the phone keeps ringing. I sit back down on the floor and pick up a license plate from the box. These are special plates that Babe has collected for years. Some of them belonged to her daddy's collection, some she found on junked cars, some she even bought. You think old license plates ain't worth nothing? Ask Babe. She is an expert on license plates. She used to belong to the License Plate Collecting Club of America. She knows all about them. Some are worth a bundle of money. License plates, Babe says, can be good business. She says people have made lots of money just by finding one rare plate. Some old plates with only a number one are rare; some with mistakes printed on them are worth quite a bit of money. Every plate, though, in good condition, is worth something.

Babe says to me, "Matchit, can you believe the United States once made plates out of soybeans?" She explained how in World War II every scrap of metal had to be used for tanks and bullets. They couldn't waste it on license plates. The only problem with soybeans was that goats and cows chewed the license plates right off people's cars. Soybean plates are worth a lot of money if you can find one.

Mostly people in prisons made these plates. What I'm wondering is were the prisoners the ones who figured out to put a pine tree on Oregon? Did they decide to put a rainbow on Hawaii? Who said let's put this fish on Massachusetts? Who were the people who owned these plates after they got made? Questions line up in my brain like people standing in line on triple-coupon day at the grocery store. There's too many to count.

Babe says old license plates turn up everywhere, in old barns, in dump grounds, in caves. Plates have even been found inside shark stomachs. Do you believe that? I don't know if I do or don't. How did a car get in the ocean? Now that, I could research.

My brain says Hey, bad-luck boy, you got a zero on Research. Remember? You were afraid to even try. You forget that already? You forget that poet guy you were supposed to look up and write about?

No, I didn't forget. I was supposed to look up Somebody Window Homes. It's a guy who wrote this poem about a warship. I liked the poem. Especially the part about the ship's deck was red with heroes' blood, and the waves were spraying white around it. The teacher told us the ship won a lot of battles, then it wore out. The government was going to sell it for junk. She said all the school kids wanted to save it, so they collected pennies and nickels and dimes from all over the whole United States. Finally, there was enough money to fix the ship like new. You can still go see it someplace, but I forgot where.

Every kid in the whole fifth grade was supposed to do research and also memorize the poem "Old Ironsides." You had to say it out loud in front of the teacher for a major grade, which is something that gets wrote down four times in the grade book.

I memorized it, too, all the way from the first line that

starts *Aye tear her tattered ensign down* to the last line that says *give her to the God of storm the lightning and the gale.* But when I got up to the teacher's desk, my brain said Hey, loser boy, you know you'll forget everything after the word *Aye.* Your skinny legs will be shaking in your shoes, and you'll make a big fool out of yourself.

"I ain't saying no stupid poem." I said it loud enough for anyone to hear. I also said I didn't mind taking four zeroes. Each one got wrote down in a little square in the teacher's book. I know because the teacher showed me.

"Do you understand how much these zeroes hurt your grade?" she asked. "Right now, your average is so low that if you mix it with your failing averages from the first and second six weeks, multiply by two, then you add your final exam grade, which will probably be failing at the rate you are going, then divide by seven, what do you have? A failing grade for the whole semester. Do you want to fail?" I didn't answer that question. I walked to my desk and sat down. I also took out the picture I drew of that ship. I tore it up in little bitty pieces like confetti. While the other kids said that poem, I dropped those pieces of paper to the floor, one by one.

After the memorizing grade, came the research. I could've done that. Only problem is that Window Homes got three paragraphs of big words in the *World Book Encyclopedia.* How am I supposed to figure out what to write down? And besides, all that stuff is boring. What I want to know is what made him care about that ship so much?

The encyclopedia don't tell that. My brain says Go ahead, bad-luck boy, take another big fat zero. You're going to fail anyway. So I did.

When you're busy washing license plates, you get a lot of things running through your brain. Some of it ain't so good. I'm washing Louisiana when the telephone rings.

Click. They hang up.

I wash two more license plates, one Arkansas and one New Mexico, and it rings again.

It's Sister. "Matthew? Ask Babe if she wants me to bring bean dip or cheese dip tonight."

"She's out walking on her stilts." I don't bother reminding her about my name.

"Oh," she says. "Well, it's your birthday. Which kind of dip do you want?"

My brain's saying You don't want any kind of dip she's poked her fingers in.

"Cat got your tongue?"

I say, "No." I ain't letting nobody or nothing get my tongue. Especially Sister.

"I'll bring both kinds of dips."

What has Babe done? She got a woman who puts her fingers in a dead squirrel's belly making dip for my birthday? One thing I wish. I wish my daddy would show up before I have to eat dinner.

I get the whole box of license plates washed and stacked. There's 320 plates, all colors, bright and shiny. I'm going to make some pretty good money for cleaning these. Plus, I like these plates. When the last cake buzzer rings, Babe comes in for good. She's done with the stilts, and she's got a scraped elbow to prove it.

She pays me the money for washing the plates, then says, "I'll listen for the phone. You run on. Do whatever you want, read, whatever."

Read? That woman's got to be kidding. I quit on the fisherman book. Besides, Dog is well. He don't need no more pages read to him.

The afternoon goes by so slow. It acts like it's driving in a school zone. I stay in my van with the windows open and the fan turned on just waiting for the day to pass. I got my shirt off. It ain't too bad. Now that I've got this place cleaned up, it's nice. I got a real artist drawing pad, which Babe brought me a few days ago, some real artist pencils, and a book about drawing. This all happened because she walked in my room one day and saw a picture of Dog I accidentally forgot to put under the bed. She made me let her put it on the refrigerator. Next thing you know, she shows up with art supplies.

I'm drawing a picture of a giant fish when she knocks on the windshield.

"Sugar," she hollers, "I got a phone call. Your surprise is almost here." She's grinning with excitement. "Don't come inside yet. Okay?" Her eyes are twinkling and I know she don't want me to spoil everything by coming in too early.

After a while I hear a car engine. Or truck. I put on my shirt, go outside, and look around. I do definitely hear something driving up to the front. It's got a bad muffler just like the one in our truck. My heart is beating faster. After the engine dies down and sputters, a door slams. Bam. Clunk. Exactly like our truck door. I can't wait no longer. No matter what Babe says, I'm going. See for myself who is there.

I'm almost up to the house when Babe comes out. She's wearing one of those pointed party hats with an elastic string under her chin. I hope she don't think I'm wearing one of those. I ain't. No way.

"There's somebody waiting for you in the kitchen," she says.

My legs feel like rubber.

"You're trembling, Matchit. What's the matter?"

"Nothing."

"Don't worry. You're going to like your surprise."

Babe ain't never lied to me.

I take a deep breath and follow her up to the house.

Chapter
NINETEEN

"CLOSE YOUR EYES," BABE ORDERS when we get around the house to the front door.

She pulls me inside. "Keep them closed," she says, leading me down the hall. I can smell the birthday cakes, but when we get to the kitchen door, I smell something else, something familiar. My heart is swinging inside my chest like a yo-yo. It's walking the dog all the way to my stomach before it jerks back up again.

I've been around that smell every day of my life nearly.

It's Menthol Man After Shave, Daddy's favorite. I'd recognize it anywhere.

"Keep those eyes shut," Babe warns. "We're almost inside." I'm not looking, but I'm trying to smell past the cakes, past the chocolate icing, straight to Daddy.

I hear the sound of a chair scraping on the linoleum, the sound of ice clinking against a glass.

"Okay. Open."

My birthday surprise is sitting at the kitchen table.

She's swirling the ice around in a glass of tea. She is so skinny and white she looks like something that got left underneath a house too long. I recognize her, though.

"Come give your mama a little hug," she says. I know she is hoping like Christmas that I will be glad to see her.

She wants to know if I remember how many creases were in my legs and arms the day she brought me home from the hospital and if I am her own little birthday boy. Don't she know I'm not a baby?

I look behind me. Babe is standing at the door watching. Does she think it's a joke telling me I got a special surprise coming, and it's just my mama, who don't have a clue about nothing? My mama, who got to have a wet washrag on her forehead every morning, who can't even remember hardly to comb her hair. It's my mama, who don't even notice how my heart is pounding, how I got sweat rolling down my face, dripping off my arms. My insides are Jell-O.

"Come here, baby," she urges me.

Babe gives me a push. "I'll leave you two alone," she says as she goes back down the hall.

Mama stands up beside the kitchen table and holds out her arms. "Please?"

When I don't move, she walks toward me. She's saying something about her precious baby, how good it is to see me, all the usual. Her voice sounds swollen, but when she gets close, her breath smells clean like peppermint.

Maybe she finally quit smoking. I always tried to get her to quit, or at least slow down. One time I drew red lines on each cigarette in the whole carton. I told her to stop smoking at the red line because after that, you get most of the dangerous stuff. She never paid any attention.

"I thought I smelled Menthol Man," I say.

"Your daddy still wears that?" She holds her arm to her nose and smells. "Maybe it's my lotion. It does sort of remind me of his aftershave. Want to smell?" She holds her arm out to me.

I shake my head. There's no point. She's not Daddy.

"Come here, Matchit." She reaches out for me again. I stiffen up, but I let her pull me close to her for a few seconds. Her blouse presses against my cheek, and for once she smells fresh. She smells like spray starch. Then she starts to cry.

My brain says Matchstick, you always do it. You always make your mama cry. Remember the last time you saw her? It was Thanksgiving at Ruby's Cafeteria, and all she did was tell you to put your napkin in your lap and to mind your manners. And you told her . . . well, you remember what you said. You didn't think she had any right to act like a regular mother. She cried right there in the cafeteria in front of all those people. Remember? You're worse than pig pee, boy.

I tell my brain to shut up. My mama cries because she wants something, because she don't want something. She cries because it's easy.

Today, sitting at Babe's table, she reaches into her

purse for a Kleenex. She wipes her nose, then looks me in the face with her dark brown eyes, so dark they look black. "It's so good to see you, Matchit," she says.

I don't say nothing.

She brushes her hand across the side of her face and sticks a sprig of hair that's fallen out of her ponytail behind her ear.

"I stood in line five hours to buy a Powerball ticket," she tells me. "If I'd won that lottery, I would have bought you a whole toy store for your birthday."

I put my hands in my pockets and wait. I'm bored already.

"Well, I wish I could have won you something," she says.

"How did you know I was here?"

"Your daddy called me the other night from Rapid City."

Now, that gets my attention.

"He said the way it's going, with his truck and all, it could be a good bit longer before he can make it back. He said to tell you that he sure is sorry. He feels terrible about not being here for your birthday."

If I act disappointed, she will think it is all her fault because that is exactly how she thinks about everything, so I tell her that I'm fine. I don't care if he's here or not. It's okay staying in a junkyard. There ain't no rats or nothing.

"So what have you been doing lately?" she asks.

"Not much."

My brain says You going to tell her you built a tunnel, you been reading to a pigeon?

I shake my head and say, "Not much of anything."

"I wish I could take you home with me." Then I know she's about to add the part she always says, the part about she has a whole lot of room in her heart for me, but everything else is too crowded. She don't say it. She got no excuses.

Next, she wants me to stand next to her so she can see how tall I am. She pulls herself up out of the chair and measures with her hand how far the top of my head comes to her shoulder and past. I'm at the bottom of her ear, at least. "You're getting so tall," she says. "How'd that happen?"

I just press my lips together and wait for the next questions. She will want to know the usual, even though it is summer. How am I doing in school? I will say fine. Am I being good? I will say yes. But before she has a chance to ask those questions, Babe walks in.

"Well, sugar, what do you think about your big surprise?"

I glance toward my mama. It's not what I expected.

"It looks like your mother brought you a present." Babe nods toward the gift bag on the table. She is reminding me to have good manners, to pay attention to what Mama done. I pick up the sack, which is decorated with reindeer and elves and has green-and-red tissue paper sticking out the top. My mama don't know if it's July or Christmas.

"Go ahead. Open it," Mama says, grinning up at Babe. I pick up the gift, which is so lightweight it don't seem like nothing. It's also squishy. That means socks or underwear.

A soft package is never a portable CD player or a Game Boy, that's for sure. I pull out the tissue and the first thing I see is one of those little metal cars, the kind I played with when I was five. I set the car down and feel to the bottom of the sack, which holds something soft, just like I thought it would. What's going to be next? Pajamas with feet?

I pull away the tissue paper, and sure enough it's clothes, a shirt. Nobody in my school wears Hawaiian shirts with big green coconut trees on a blue background. I don't plan on ever going to Hawaii, plus it looks way too small. Still, I button it on over my T-shirt. It just barely comes to the top of my jeans.

I tug at the bottom to make it seem to fit better. "This is nice," I say politely. I expect her to cry because I messed up by being too big, but she don't. She laughs. "I didn't know you had grown so much. You should've warned me!"

I shake my head because there is so much she does not know about me. It would take too long to explain.

Babe says that when Sister and Zebby arrive, there will be more surprises. Zebby's taken a pickup truck to get Sister and something else. She won't say what the something else is, of course. But she is as excited as a kid. You'd think it was her birthday.

Mama seems happy, too. She brags on the twelve-layer cake, which is so tall it's leaning to one side. She wants to see Dog when Babe mentions him, and when Babe carries him into the kitchen in his cage and he's wearing a tiny birthday hat, Mama laughs. She can't quit laughing, it seems like. She talks about how pretty Dog is, how his feathers feel soft as a kitten's fur, and she puts her face to the bars on his cage and talks to him just like I do. She asks him if I am being good, if I am minding my manners and helping out. When he steps closer to the bars, which I know means he wants a sunflower seed, she laughs. She tells him she is glad her son got a friend. "Keep an eye on Matchit," she says. "I love him very much."

Finally, she says she's had a nice time, but she's got to go. She can't wait for Sister and Zebby because it will get dark soon. "I don't feel confident driving at night," she says. "Even with my new glasses." She pulls a pair of eyeglasses from her purse and puts them on. "How do I look?" she asks me. "I bet you never thought your mother would worry about a little thing like driving in the dark, did you?"

Babe tells me to walk her out to her car, that she'll give Sister a call, find out when she and Zebby will be coming over with my next surprise.

I follow Mama out to the car, and when we get there, she kisses me on the cheek thirteen times, one for each year I've been alive plus one to grow on. Thirteen is an unlucky number, but I don't say nothing because something about my mama seems a little bit lucky. She seems different than I've ever seen her before, stronger. Daddy always says she is like one of those dandelion puffs, the kind that break apart so easy, and before you know it, pieces are flying everywhere. Today Mama don't seem like she'd break apart so easy.

"I really do love you," she says, standing at the car door.

I nod. I love you is something I don't say to nobody, especially somebody who might forget all about smelling good, who might forget to get out of bed tomorrow.

"How do you like my new car?" she asks. "It's not really new, of course, but it's new to me. I bought it myself. Can you believe it?"

I don't know whether to believe it or not, but it looks like a pretty good car. It's a Toyota, and it's probably got a lot of miles on it, but the tires look good, plenty of tread. Inside, the seats aren't torn or nothing. It surprises me it's a standard instead of an automatic.

"You learned how to drive a stick?" I ask.

She grins. "I've been learning a lot of things, Matchit. Life doesn't have any shortcuts. That's one thing. I have some choices. That's another. And I can't redo the past. That's the most important."

She leans against her car and looks up. The sun is going down and everywhere you look almost, the sky is striped with orange. "I'm in a group that helps me a lot. We meet every night, nearly, and I have a day job at the junior college in the business office. I file and do some book work. I'm even going to sign up for a class, maybe. I'll be sending your daddy child support payments, too. There's so much to do. It seems like I don't have enough time for everything. Used to be, I had too much time." She puts her hand on my shoulder and reminds me that even though she can't take care of me right now, she might be able to sometime.

141

I say I better go in. Babe's waiting.

"Matchit? I want you to know something. Just in case you've wondered." She bites her bottom lip and takes a deep breath. "I want you to know that when I left, when you were a baby, it wasn't about you or your daddy. It was about me."

I don't ask questions. I just watch her car drive off. I don't wave or nothing.

Chapter
TWENTY

"THIS BIKE IS REALLY MINE?" Babe has just pushed a brand-new silver freestyle with silver pegs into the kitchen.

"It's sure not mine," Babe says. "I've never ridden a bike in my life. Now Sister, you'll have to watch *her*. She might take it away from you."

Sister frowns. "You better like the color," she grumbles. "It's all they had down at Rice's Hardware."

"I do," I tell her. I like silver. I like everything about this bike. You can do a lot of tricks on a bike like this. I even like the helmet, which is silver and is hanging from the handlebars.

I run my hands down the chrome handlebars, try out the hand brakes. I can't believe this. This bike is brand new.

Babe says since I probably already have a bicycle at home, I can leave this one at the junkyard for when I come to visit. "Or you can take it home and have two bikes," she adds.

I tell her I might do that. She don't have to know I never had a bike of my own.

"I got it for him to run errands," Sister announces. "Earn his keep around here. He can go to the store or ride over and help me out when I need it. He's getting too spoiled over here."

Babe looks at me and grins.

"You like it?"

I nod.

"You'll have to wait until tomorrow to ride it," Babe says. "You'll want it to be light out to make sure you don't run over any nails or anything."

"Okay," I tell her. It is finally sinking into my brain that this bike is mine. All mine. Suddenly, I remember my manners. "Thank you," I say.

"That's enough," Sister announces. "Just don't start thinking I'm going to buy you something every time you turn around. You hear? And be careful riding that thing."

"Yes ma'am," I answer. At the same time my brain's trying to remind me about something secret, something I don't want to think about. I shake my head.

"What's the matter, sugar?" Babe asks.

"Nothing," I tell her. There is something big that's bothering me, but I make myself smile and when I do, she brings out three more presents. One is from Zebby. It's a drawing.

"Let us see," Babe says.

I hold it up. It's a drawing of a boy on a bicycle sailing over a junkyard full of cars. The boy looks a lot like me. My brain says Matchstick, that boy ain't you. And you know why.

"This gift is from Dog," Babe says, handing me another wrapped box. "Sister helped him pick it out. Dog said to tell you he appreciates all the reading you've been doing for him. He says back when he was real sick, he stayed alive just to find out what would happen on the next page."

I look over at Dog. He ain't paying no attention and Sister is shaking her head.

Sister picked out this present? I hope it ain't dead. I open it real slow, scraping at the tape with my fingernails, pulling slow on the ribbon. I peel off the paper. It's a wood-burning kit, which does look like fun maybe. You can burn pictures into wood, make signs, whatever you want. Sister wants to plug it in and burn something right now, but Babe puts her off, says it's my kit and that Sister can get her own. I tell Dog thank you.

The third gift is from Babe and she's excited about it. She even cuts the ribbon to help me go faster. When I open the box, I am really surprised. My mouth just about falls open. I can't believe it.

"It's your license plate collection," I whisper. I'm remembering she told me that some of these plates could be worth a lot of money, hundreds of dollars maybe.

Babe hands me a license plate collector's catalog. "Here," she says, "you can study this to see what everything's worth. You can sell them if you want to. Do whatever you want. They're yours."

I try to give back the money she paid me for cleaning them, but she won't hear a thing of it. "I couldn't give you dirty plates for your birthday, could I?"

Sister shakes her head and complains that I am really, really getting spoiled, and Babe scolds her that I am loved, not spoiled. This is all embarrassing to me, but I know they are halfway playing and teasing each other. My bicycle is shining in the middle of the kitchen. It is a trophy that I didn't do nothing to win. Except getting born. Tonight I feel a little bit lucky.

Even though I'm disappointed Daddy didn't come, I know he'll call. When he does, I'll tell him about the bike and other things, and he'll say, "You got that bicycle in bed with you?" When I was little, I slept with anything new that I got. I slept with my new shoes beside me on the pillow, slept with a new box of crayons, a toy John Deere tractor and trailer, a toy Zebco fishing rod.

Bedtime, Daddy hasn't called yet. I'm pretty sure he's waiting until 11:16, the exact time I was born twelve years ago. I wheel my bike into the bedroom and park it next to the bed. I ain't sleeping with no bicycle. I lie in bed looking at it and waiting for the telephone to ring. At 11:18, he still hasn't called. 12:01. All his chances are gone. My birthday is over for another year. I turn off the light.

You think I'm going to lie here on my back and cry? I ain't crying about nothing. I squeeze my eyes shut as hard

146

as I can. I warn them. You better not have one tear or you're in trouble. It's too late. I sit up, grab my pillow, and throw it into the dark as hard as I can. It crashes into my bike, which falls onto the floor with a loud bang.

Dog beats his wings against the side of the cage, and I shine my flashlight on his long red skinny toes. I tell him I don't care about the bike. I don't care about Daddy. I don't care about nothing. My words stab me in the heart.

Ha! You really thought your daddy would remember your birthday? He's clear across the country. And one more thing, Matchstick. About that bicycle. You know you won't be riding no bike.

Shut up, I say into the darkness.

My brain don't ever give up, not even when I'm feeling low already.

I lean my bike against the foot of the bed. And I tell Dog I'm sorry for scaring him. I lie down and turn my face to the wall.

My brain keeps on. You could be in the *Guinness Book of World Records,* Matchstick McCarty. Oldest boy in the world who don't know how to ride a bike.

Chapter
TWENTY-ONE

I WAKE UP LATE THE NEXT MORNING.

"Matchit?" Babe is talking to me through the door. "The mail came. You've got something."

I pull on my jeans and shirt and open the door. She hands me a long white envelope. Inside there's two things. One is a postcard of Mount Rushmore. On the back is wrote: *Carved in stone. That's how my love is for you.* The other thing is a piece of cardboard with a ten-dollar bill and four fifty-cent pieces taped on the front. On the back Daddy wrote: "Jewel gave me this idea. She's a real gem, Match. Ha! Ha!"

"Why don't you ride your bike down to Lucky's, spend some of your money?" Babe asks.

"Maybe," I answer.

Babe gives me a funny look. "Aren't you anxious to try out your bike?"

148

My mouth is dry. My heart beats fast and hard. It seems like my secret is shining right through my chest, bright and lit up like Christmas lights for everyone to see.

"You know how hand brakes work, don't you?"

I nod as I slip into my shoes. I squat down to tie them, trying to think of a way out. She will want to watch me on my bike, watch me ride out the drive.

"Hand brakes are nothing," I tell her. "I'm just in the mood for walking."

Babe gives me a look that says she don't quite believe me, but she don't say nothing.

All the way to Lucky's, I kick rocks, sticks, anything. I kick every one in sight that's too big for its britches. One kick for my daddy, one for Jake, for Jewel, for the bike I can't ride, for everybody and everything I know, even a kick for the sun that is shining way too hot.

You can't sneak into Lucky's. They got a cowbell tied to the door.

At first when I walk in, I don't see nobody. What I smell is barbecue from a smoker out back of the kitchen. They got all kinds of food in this little store, chopped beef sandwiches, smoked pig knuckles, buffalo wings. There's a two-gallon jar full of pickled eggs and gallon jars of beef jerky, cherry peppers, and jalapeños.

"You that boy staying out at Babe's place?"

Huh? Somebody talking to me? I hear his voice, but I don't see him at first. He's squatting behind the counter stacking up boxes of cigarettes.

"I've heard about you," he says, standing up.

What's he heard? I don't do my homework? I leave all the blanks empty on my tests? I'm in Slow and Dumb, not Gifted and Talented? Maybe he heard I got dumped in a junkyard and he's going to call Child Protective Services. With people like this, it's better if you don't say too much.

I walk toward the back of the store, toward the refrigerated drink case. They got canned soft drinks, bottled water, beer, whatever you want.

"You looking to buy a can of beer?" he jokes. He's a big guy with a big stomach that flops over his belt like a deflated inner tube. He reminds me of Jake.

I shake my head on the beer. I tasted my mama's one time. It about made me puke. The way they make beer is they put a whole bunch of rotten things in a barrel, chicken bones, anything they can think of. Then they let it sit until it gets smelly and moldy, then they pour off the juice and add water. That's why my daddy don't drink it. Can't stand the stuff. Now, Jake, he'd eat a dead worm if somebody put it on his plate.

This guy watches me like a hawk. He think I'm going to steal something? I got a whole pocket full of money, and I reach in to pull out a ten-dollar bill.

Besides my money from Daddy, I got the money Babe gave me for the plates. I can buy anything I want.

I walk over to the game in the corner. You think Lucky's has video games? It don't. They got pinball, though.

"Can you give me some quarters?" I ask, handing him one of the fives Babe gave me for cleaning the plates.

150

"Five dollars' worth?"

I nod.

He puts the quarters in a cup and hands it to me. He's looking at me like he don't trust me.

I win two games, which gives you one free, and shooting those marbles through a maze that winds up in a dragon's mouth is almost as fun as video games. I stand at that game for a long time, spending quarters.

"You don't give up easily, do you?" It's the store worker. He's standing behind me.

"What?"

"That pinball game. I bet you are a good student, the way you work at a thing so hard."

That guy, he don't know nothing. I pour the rest of the quarters out of the cup into my pocket.

I walk over to the fountain area where the cups and soft drink machines are. There are a lot of choices. You can get a large cup, which costs a dime more than the extra extra large, which is called the Giant Gulp. They got a special on those. I take down one of those cups. You could pour a half-gallon of milk in one of those things. I'm still getting watched, even while I press the cup against the ice dispenser.

I want to mix a squirt of everything, Root Beer, Lemon-Lime, RC, Big Red, the whole line, but he's got the evil eye on me, and I figure he won't like it. So what? I do it anyway.

That guy never saw a kid fill a cup before? He's even watching while I press the lid on top and poke the straw through the hole. I walk to the aisle with the candy and other snacks. They got a lot to choose from, but finally I pick up a box of Cracker Jacks. You think I care about the surprise inside? I don't.

He follows me to the counter, where there's a basket that says Lucky Key Chains $3.99. Each one has a lucky four-leaf clover pressed into a clear piece of plastic. A four-leaf clover is something I've always looked for. You can look through a million fields of grass and not find one.

"So have you been having fun out at Babe's? She's a nice lady."

"It's okay."

"You like those key chains?"

Before I have a chance to answer, the phone rings. He answers and says he needs to go to the back to check on something. He wants to know if I'll watch the counter for a minute.

When he's gone, I take Daddy's late birthday note out of my pocket and read it again. If I turned into a criminal or something, he'd be sorry. Sorry he took off and left me. Sorry he didn't keep his promise and at least call on my birthday.

The man is still in the back. I hear him moving around boxes.

I pick up one of those four-leaf clover key chains and look at it up close. It does look like the real thing.

I could pay for it. I have the money, but that's not the point. I don't even take time to think no more. I shove the key chain into my pocket.

I never stole anything in my whole life. My mouth feels dry. My hands feel shaky. Is this how you feel when you turn into a criminal?

"Sorry. It took me a little longer than I thought it would."

I just about jump out of my skin. I didn't hear him come up behind me.

"Thanks for helping me out."

I nod, looking down. It seems like he can see right through my pocket. Can he tell there's one key chain missing?

"What is your name, anyway?"

I freeze. Why does he want to know? I clear my throat.

"Oliver," I say. The name just pops into my head. Then I add, "Oliver Homes."

The guy don't even blink. "Oliver. Nice to meet you. So, how old are you? I got a nephew about your age."

"Fourteen."

"Tell your parents they raised a mighty nice boy."

I got to get out of here. I pay for my drink and Cracker Jacks and rush out the door. I don't even glance back.

Outside I don't hear nothing. Nothing, that is, except my brain. It's saying Oliver Window Homes better be glad he got a window in his name, because one of these days when he's sitting in his jail cell, he'll be glad he got one to look out.

I start to run.

I'm almost fifty yards down the road when I hear the holler. "Wait! Come back!"

I run harder. After a while the voice gets lost in the air, and I keep running as hard as I can. Suddenly, I feel him behind me, at my heels, galloping in those big shoes of his, his long arms about to grab me, and I keep running like a swarm of yellow jackets is after me.

My chest hurts I'm running so hard. Matchstick, you got enough scary pictures in your head to fill up a movie theater. You too chicken to turn around and look?

Finally, I glance back.

It's Zebby. He's standing in the middle of the road watching me.

Chapter
TWENTY-TWO

WHEN I GET BACK TO BABE'S, I hide the lucky key chain inside the back door panel in the van. Two days pass and nobody calls reporting what I done. Zebby don't say nothing, either. I figure if he knows, he's not telling or else he's planning to blackmail me later. Babe acts the same as ever, cheerful, talking a mile a minute. It's clear she don't know nothing. Except about the bike. On that she don't let up.

She walks out to the van one morning while I'm working on hanging my three-way light. "Matchit," she says, leaning her head into the van window. "I haven't seen you out riding your bike. I thought you'd be building ramps by now, pedaling downtown, riding in the middle of the night. You haven't even rolled it down the hallway." She asks me, "You sure you don't want another color? I have plenty of paint."

"It's fine." I don't want to talk about my bike.

"Is it big enough? Do we need to move the seat up or down to fit you better?" She explains how I ought to be able to straighten my legs while I'm sitting on the seat. "If you have to bend your knees, we need to move the seat up."

I'm staring at my fingernails because I can't tell her the truth.

Babe opens the van door and sits down. She's looking at the door panel. Right where that stolen key chain is hidden. I feel my throat get tight.

"Something troubling you, Matchit? If it is, you can tell me." She quits talking and stares out across the junkyard. I ain't saying nothing.

Finally, she lets out a big sigh.

"I would love to ride that bicycle of yours. But here I am, all grown up, and I never learned to ride one of those things. Can you believe that?"

Yes, I can. That's what happens when you don't learn when you're young like you're supposed to. You get old and the wish of riding a bike wrinkles up in your brain and stays there. You always remember and you always feel bad. You feel like a kindergartner is smarter than you are.

"Matchit?" Babe says. "Would you let me try to ride your bicycle? I think I could still learn."

My brain sees right through what she's trying to do. She's going to fake it that she can't ride a bike because she thinks that will make me try, too. The only difference between her and the testing lady at school is that Babe don't have a pocket full of cartoon pencils to make me try harder.

"So will you let me use your bike to try?" she asks.

"Might as well," I mumble.

We walk back up to the house, where my bike is still sitting next to the bed. I roll it out the door and follow Babe out on the road. Babe straps on the helmet, which fits her pretty good. She says, "I'll get on the thing. After that, you put your hand on the back of the seat, give me a push. Hard as you can!"

Babe gets on the bike, but the seat is way too little. Parts of her hang over the sides, but she don't care. She puts one foot on a pedal, the other on the ground. "I think I'm ready," she says. "Now, push!"

You got to be kidding. This joke is going too far, but I put my hand on the back of the seat. Pushing Babe's like trying to push a diesel truck with your bare hands. It ain't easy. At first, she don't budge at all. I tell her to help me, to push with the foot she's still got on the ground. She does that and I shove her as hard as I can. She puts both feet on the pedals, and hollers for me to let go. For a few seconds, maybe two or three, she's pedaling hard even though the front wheel is wobbling back and forth totally out of control. The next thing I know, she's in the dirt.

When she gets up, her elbow is bleeding in a long red streak down her arm. She picks a pebble out of the middle of the bloody scrape, then brushes the rest of the dirt off her legs and arms. She grins at me. "How was that?"

She's not about to act like she made a mistake. She'll be more careful the next time. I figure she'll try a couple of more times to make it look good, then ride like she's been doing it all her life.

"I'm trying again," which is what I knew she'd say. "Any advice?" she asks.

If she's going to pretend, I am too. "You got to hold the handlebars straight, don't turn them to the sides," I tell her. "Use your feet to balance, and don't look back at me. Try to hold still and look ahead. Oh yeah, one more thing: Pedal harder." I got directions coming out my mouth like an instruction manual. What's the matter with me? My brain thinks it knows how to ride a bicycle?

She says I got good advice, and she swings her leg over the seat and gets back on. "Don't hold on to me this time," she says. "I'm going to try to hold the handlebars straight, get my balance, and ride down to the end of the road where the mailbox sits."

This time she keeps one foot on the ground for a longer time, steadying herself, and pushing with the other foot, like she's riding a scooter. Finally, she puts both feet on the pedals. She goes about three feet, makes a big crazy eight with the handlebars, and I see her heading straight for the ditch on the side of the road. Next thing I know, she's down.

I run over to the ditch and she is just lying there in the weeds, one leg twisted under the bike wheel, her face scrunched up in pain.

"Ouch!" she says, smiling up at me. "Can you lift the

bike off?" After I lift it off of her, she stands up real slow and checks her knee. It's scraped pretty good and there's a knot already rising up as big as an egg. "It's a little bit harder than I thought it would be," she says. She looks up to the sky. "And that hot sun isn't giving me any help."

"Want to quit?" I ask. That knee of hers is going to have a scab as big as Texas.

"You kidding? I've lost too much blood to waste it. Besides, this time I just about got it."

This woman is crazy. She don't give up for nothing. She is walking with a limp, and she's bleeding from both her knee and elbow, but she tucks her T-shirt into her pants and brushes her hands together. "Third time's the charm," she says. She pushes the bike out of the ditch and back onto the road. She gets on and starts off again, and this time she makes it partway down the road. She's still making crazy eights with the handlebars, and not on purpose, but she is managing to stay on. Then she turns to wave at me. Big mistake.

This time it's her lip. A big blob of red is running down her chin. By the time I get to her, her lip is swollen, and it's so bloody I can't tell if she cut the top or bottom. Her whole lip might be gone for all I can tell. She's still smiling, sort of, but she also has tears in the corners of her eyes. You'd think she'd decide to quit, but she don't. This woman is even more determined now. She gets on the bike, pushes herself off with her feet, and rides down the road again. This time, she goes down the road a few feet farther before she falls.

"Didn't even hurt myself this time," she shouts back at me. She tries again. Picking up speed, she hollers, "Here goes!" Both feet are on the pedals now, and for a few seconds she's riding. Then it's over. I run to her and help her onto her feet again.

I'm about to tell her to give it up, but I know she won't quit. She'll keep falling and trying again, over and over until she pedals down the road. Finally, it happens. She's swerving from one side to the other, but she's staying up, and she's hollering like crazy. "Whoopee! Here I go! Watch me, Matchit! I'm riding!" It's embarrassing. She's as bad as a little kid. She rides past me down to the mailbox and back again.

She climbs off the bike and hands it to me. "I did it!" she says, panting for breath. She wipes the fresh blood from her lip with the back of her arm and spits the rest into the dirt.

My brain says Matchstick, you loser boy. Even a woman old enough to be a grandmother can ride a bike.

Babe says, "You know what I think, Matchit? There's a boy inside you who is expert at riding bicycles. It's a done deal. All you have to do is let him come out."

I look at her like she's crazy, and before I know it, the words are shooting out of my mouth. "I can ride it if I want to. I don't want to. I got a whole lot better bike than this at home. My dad bought it. I ride it all over the place. It can fly over any ramp, any hill you want."

"My," she says, "no wonder you don't want to ride this plain old bicycle."

I nod in agreement, and she says I sure don't have to ride it if I don't want to. She's going into the house to clean up. After she's gone, I think about getting on that bike. Nobody would see.

But I don't want to. I don't care about riding no bike, this one especially. It's an especially dumb bike. I give the front tire a hard kick. Then I put one hand on each handle grip and stand beside it.

I give it a push with my hands and I start walking. I walk that bike all the way back to the house. The farther I walk, the madder I get. I figure it's Babe's fault. And Sister's. They don't have the right to get me nothing.

I feel like beating somebody up.

After supper, Babe goes over to Sister's. I'm just sitting around. The phone rings.

The first thing I hear after I say hello is "Did you get your birthday card? Did you get the money?"

Daddy acts like nothing even happened.

"You said you'd call," I answer. "You didn't."

"I'm sorry, Matchit."

I twist the cord around my finger. "Something happen to the truck?"

He ignores that question. "Did you get the money that was in your birthday card?"

"Yeah."

"Just don't spend it all in one place," he jokes.

I don't say nothing.

"So, what have you been doing?" he asks.

"Riding my bike."

"You got a bicycle?"

"For my birthday. It's really great. Just like I always wanted. I'm riding it all over the place." My own heart squeezes up on that lie. It's a real whopper. My bike is sitting on its kickstand in my bedroom.

Daddy gets quiet for a few seconds, and as usual, I can see him with his hand cupped on his chin, rubbing the edge of his sideburn with his thumb.

"That's good, son. That's real good." He's feeling sorry he didn't buy me a bike, sorry he wasn't here to watch, just like I hoped he'd feel.

"And Babe gave me a whole box of license plates. It's her private collection. They're worth a lot of money."

"Oh yeah?"

"I can sell them if I want. I can get a lot more than twelve dollars, probably twenty or thirty times that much, at least."

"I'll get you something else when I get home," he says real quiet.

"You said you'd go up to Mount Rushmore and come right back. You said you'd be here for my birthday. Then you said you'd at least call. You said you'd send Babe money. Just like you said you'd buy me a bike, but you never did." I can't stop myself.

"Yeah, Matchit, I know. I'm sorry, okay?"

I close my mouth, letting everything that is missing in my father sink into his brain. He's got ten zeroes in my grade book, and if he was sitting in a school desk, he'd be squirming.

He clears his throat and coughs. "This old truck is not going to make it. The alternator went out yesterday."

"I thought we rebuilt that thing."

"Yeah, we did. It's time for some good luck, don't you think?"

"Want me to send you a lucky key chain with a real four-leaf clover inside?" Then because he is so far away, because he already feels bad about all the ways he has messed up, I add, "I stole it."

"What are you talking about?"

I tell him I was at Lucky's. There was a basket of these key rings, and I just took one. Put it in my pocket and walked out the door. It was easy. It was fun.

"You take that thing back," he orders. "I want you to pay for it, and I want you to apologize. Do it, or I'll have Babe take you in there herself."

"She won't. She steals stuff, too." I wait a few seconds for it to sink in. "She's the one who got me started. She stole two cigarette lighters the same day I took the key chain. She gave one of them to me, and she said she'd pay me for stealing some cartons of cigarettes. They let me smoke, too, anytime I want. Sister steals, too. She stole a whole bucket of fake eyeballs. I think that's how they got my bicycle. It was stolen. And that guy who lives in the school bus, he's been in prison before, ask Babe. He's killed people. She has a newspaper article about him. You left me in a real good place."

163

Daddy explodes. "Put Babe on the phone. Now!"

"She's gone. She left me here alone. She always does."

Daddy sighs so loud you could hear him a block away. He's partly blaming himself. He knows he's left me here too long.

"You coming to get me?"

"I'm not in the mood for joking, Match. I'm calling Jake. He'll be out to pick you up."

I slam down the phone. My day has turned into one royal mess.

Chapter
TWENTY-THREE

THE NEXT DAY I'M IN MY ROOM ON THE PORCH when I hear a loud roar coming up the front drive. My stomach falls down to my ankles.

Next comes a pounding at the door. There's only one person who always does that. I hear heavy boots clomp across the tile in the front room. Finally, I hear a loud booming voice.

"I'm telling you, Arnie sent me out here. He called and said I'm supposed to get the boy. The kid knows all about it, too. Didn't he bother to tell you?"

"I need verification," Babe is saying. "I'm not letting Matchit go without it. Besides, we want Matchit to stay."

"I don't have no verifi—whatever. And you probably can't get ahold of Arnie. He's on a job site somewhere."

"Well then, Matchit's not going anywhere."

"I come all the way out here, riding in this scorching heat. I ain't leaving without the boy."

"He's not *the boy*. He has a name. Matchit."

"You might not like him so much if you heard what he told his daddy. About you. That's the main reason I'm here, as a matter of fact."

I put my pillow over my head. I can't stand to hear any more. I know Jake is telling Babe all about how I accused her of stealing. The part about Zebby being a killer I don't mind. And Sister, I don't feel so bad about calling her a thief. But Babe, she probably hasn't stole as much as a safety pin her whole life. When Babe hears all the things I said, all the trouble I've caused, she'll tell Jake to get me and fast. She won't want no crazy juvenile delinquent kid around her house.

He'll wrap his big fat fingers around my arm, tell me I still got a skinny Barbie doll muscle, tell me I don't even got hair on my arms. Then he'll make me go home with him and sleep on the cot in the kitchen. He'll stay up all night working on his motorcycle in the living room and the rest of the time he'll make my life miserable. I'll be stuck until Daddy gets back, and who knows how long that's going to be.

I got to get out of here. I head out the screen door into my tunnel. I'm crawling as fast as I can. I got dirt flying up to my face, I'm going so fast. I'll get in my van and hide. Wait. That's the first place they'll look. I've got to hide someplace else. I keep crawling, up to the van, inside, and out the passenger door. The worst car on the whole lot is an old black Plymouth. It's a big black hump of a car, looks like a stinkbug. The front windows are covered in so much grime, you can't see inside. The backseat windows are tiny slits that are just for looks, but they're black with dirt, too. Nobody would ever think a kid would get in that thing.

The front driver's door won't open, so I go around to the passenger side, where the door is barely open, hanging crooked like a broken arm. I get in and slam it shut as hard as I can.

Inside this car, the air is hot, hot as an oven, and it tastes dirty. I feel like I'm about to throw up.

Jake's not this bad, my brain tells me.

Oh no? Wait until you get one of his nuclear wedgies. You like your underwear around your chin? I ain't going with Jake for nothing.

I raise my head just enough to peek through the passenger window, which I have to spit on and rub with my hand to even see out a little.

Way across the yard is Zebby. I duck quick so he won't see me. I don't want him telling nobody where I am.

Inside this old car the front seat's missing, so I squat down on the floor. I peek out again. Zebby's still facing this way. The air is getting hotter and hotter. It's so hot, my chest is starting to hurt.

I reach to roll down a window, but there's one big problem. Somebody's already screwed off all the knobs.

My face hurts. My chest hurts, too. This air is so thick, so hot.

Think, Matchit. You're suffocating. You ever heard stories about dogs getting locked in a hot car on a hot day? They die. You better get some air, boy.

I crawl to the door.

It won't open. No matter what I do, it won't budge.

Sweat's rolling out my hair and down onto my face like someone's poured a bucket of water on my head. It's running salty on my lips, pushing its way into my mouth. It wants to choke me, too.

It's so hot, I don't ever remember being so hot.

Matchstick, you slow boy. You're stuck in a car without no air. Don't you know what's going to happen? Your blood will start to cook, baking up hard as a cement sidewalk. Pretty soon, no matter how hard you try, you won't be able to get a crack of air inside your lungs.

I try to take a breath. Sure enough, only a thread of air gets in.

I shove the door hard as I can. It still won't open.

If I don't get out of here, I will die.

My hands are grabbing at the window, pushing on the glass trying to claw it open. My eyes are burning. I can't see so good, and I figure they're about to cook, too. They'll be as hard as marbles.

I squint to see a blur in the distance. It's Jake. He's carrying his fish-boning knife.

He's coming closer and closer, almost up to the car. I wipe the back of my hand across my eyes and take another look.

I see the fasteners on his overalls, and the fish-boning knife ain't a knife. It's a crowbar. It's not Jake. It's Zebby.

My insides are quivering, and my brain's saying which do you want, Matchit, be found and have to go with Jake, or suffocate?

I don't have time to decide. The heat's got its fingers around my throat. It's squeezing me hard, then harder and harder. I hear my fists beating on the glass, pounding harder and harder, slapping, tearing at the windows.

Zebby's moving fast toward the car.

He's got a wild look in his eyes, and he's coming at me, swooping down on me, hammering on the door. He rips the door off the hinges like a crazy man. I'm falling outside, and I hear myself screaming.

It's a loud shrieking scream that don't want to quit.

Next thing, I feel big hands pulling me up off the ground, standing me up. I take off.

I'm running for my life, through weeds, over tires, over piled-up junk, falling and ripping my knee on a jagged edge of something, running until I get to the house, jerk open the door to my room on the porch, and lock it.

My brain says Look what you gone and done, you big baby.

I look down at myself.

You're some kind of sissy boy, Matchstick. All tough on the outside, something else on the inside.

Jake will be waiting for me. I know it. And if he sees me, he will never let me forget that I got so scared I wet my pants.

Chapter TWENTY-FOUR

MATCHSTICK, you are one lying, stealing, skinny-butt, bad-luck kid. You better give up. You got nowhere else to hide. Go straight to the bathroom, take a shower, and dress in the same clothes you wore when you first came to Babe's, new jeans, button-up-the-front shirt, and almost-never-been-worn socks. Comb your hair, slick it down with water on top where the cowlicks are. You are going with Jake, like it or not.

You are also one big baby, I tell myself, and I feel the shamefulness of what I done and who I am creep from my toes to my neck.

I strip down, tie a towel around my waist, and pick up the stack of new clothes. I've got to make it to the bath-room down the hall without being heard.

Slowly, I push open the door to my room. It squeaks,

and I wish I had a can of WD-40 to make it shut up. The bathroom is just a few feet down the hall. I take one step, and the floor squeaks. Another step. It squeaks again.

"What are you doing, Barbie boy?"

Jake is standing in front of the bathroom, leaning on the door.

I tell him I'm going to take a shower and get dressed. I'm gripping that towel tight around my waist. Jake thinks it's fun to grab your towel and snap it at you while you try to hide your privates. This time, Babe walks between Jake and me. She asks him to step aside, and she opens the bathroom door.

I dash inside and turn the lock. Jake's been practicing most of his life at being a bully. It makes him feel like he's one big tough dude. Inside himself, though, I bet he ain't an inch tall.

After my shower, I put on clean clothes and stand at the mirror to comb my hair. I pull my clothes out of the dresser drawers and stuff them into my suitcase.

When I walk into the kitchen, Babe is in the hallway on the telephone. "He's got an old motorcycle that looks like it's about to fall apart." She glances at me with a worried look. "No, Sis, I can't get Arnie. Just get over here." She hangs up the phone just as Jake walks in.

"Your daddy says you haven't been behaving yourself," he says. "What's this about you stealing things? What you need is a good whipping with a belt. I'm always telling your daddy he's too easy on you. You're a little sissy pet boy, never even been spanked. Let's see what you stole, boy." I'm not looking at him, but I can feel Jake smiling because one thing he loves is telling on people.

That four-leaf clover key chain is safe in my van.

My eyes are stuck on the toes of Jake's boots. They got shiny pointed steel tips to make him look mean. I'm hoping Babe will start yelling at me, get it over with, but nobody says a word, and the toes of Jake's boots look meaner and meaner.

"I said what'd ya steal, boy? Show me."

I don't move.

"I'm taking you to my place. Somebody needs to make a man out of you."

I keep my eyes on the floor where they belong, my hands in my pockets.

I'm about to pick up my suitcase when I feel an arm wrap around my shoulder. It squeezes me tight and a voice says it don't matter if I stole something or not. It don't matter if I said bad things about her or not. She knows I didn't mean it. Babe says I'm still her gifted and talented, sweet-hearted boy.

I jerk her arm off me. She don't have no right to say that kind of lies. Go with Jake, my brain says. That's where you belong.

I take a deep breath. "I'm ready," I say to Jake. "I don't want to stay here anymore. This lady is mean. Crazy, too."

I don't look at Babe. I don't want to see if she looks hurt or not. I just want to get out of here where people think I am better than I am. The only thing is, I didn't say good-bye to Dog.

"Just a minute. I forgot something." I turn to head back to my room, but Jake stops me.

He grabs me by the arm and says, "Hey, Bubba, what'd you spill on your shirt?" I look down and he pinches my nose. I just fell for the oldest joke in the book. Jake hasn't changed a bit and I know I got a lot more teasing to dread. "Come on," he orders. "There ain't no reason for you to go back to your room. We're leaving. Now." He picks up my suitcase. "Anything you forgot, they can send you."

Like Jake says, it's time to go. Anyway, seeing Dog, that would be too hard. I lie to myself that I never stole any-thing. That I never said nothing bad about Babe, that Dog is going with me, that Jake is nice, that Daddy will drive up and I won't have to do none of this. I pretend a lot of things so that I won't be a big fat baby and cry.

When I glance up, Babe is looking straight at me. She is seeing straight into my eyes, straight into my head, all the way down to my heart.

Jake goes outside first. All the sudden, Babe runs past him. "Matchit is staying. You are not taking him." She holds out her arms like she is playing defense, man-to-man.

Jake spits into the dirt and pushes her aside. Stopping him is stopping a Mack truck going 90 per. He straps my suitcase to his bike.

"I ain't broken no laws, lady," Jake says. "This boy don't

belong to you." Jake grins because he knows he has won. Babe can't do nothing. I will end up getting on the motorcycle. I will sit behind him, and I will put my arms around his waist to hold on, even though I dread it.

Then we hear a roar. Something is coming up the road so fast, you can't even see what it is. A storm of dirt swirls up all around it.

When it gets closer, Jake lets out a long whistle. "Look at that!"

It's Sister in her cherry-red Corvette. She screeches into the drive and comes to a sudden halt. "Man!" Jake exclaims. "What a waste! A mean car like that belongs to an old chick like her?"

Sister gets out of the car in a huff. She's swinging her purse like it's something she's about to throw. She must be really mad to drive her prize Corvette through the dirt in such a hurry. "What is going on here?" she demands.

Jake has forgotten all about me, and he's not paying no attention to Sister. Now that the car is here, he's walking around it whistling at everything he sees, talking out loud to himself. He whistles at the wheels and says, "Look at them knockoffs. You got side exhaust. The paint on this 'Vette original?" He presses his face to the window and looks inside. "Leather interior, four-speed. Man! Mind if I pop the hood on this baby?"

"Yes, I mind!" Sister snaps.

"You got the big block in this thing?" Jake's wanting to know all about the engine. He don't care if Sister's upset or not. "What kind of options you got on her?"

"I've got every option anyone would ever want. Now, get your paws off of it."

Jake takes his hands off and gives her a dirty look.

I figure he would give up his prize hog tooth collection just to have a chance to drive that car to Burger Barn.

"Where's this child's motorcycle helmet?" Sister asks. She puts her purse on her shoulder and places her hands on her hips. She means business, but Jake don't care. He can't take his eyes off the Corvette. "Man, this is some machine!"

"I repeat. Where is this child's helmet?"

Jake's squatted down looking underneath the car. He's saying he don't have no helmets. He's glad because he likes to feel the wind. Besides, helmets are too hot.

Sister bends down and hollers at him under the car. "Whether you knock a hole in your fool head the size of the Grand Canyon is no concern of mine. You go right ahead and feel the wind all you want to. Children under eighteen must still wear a helmet on a motorbike."

Jake stands up real slow, looks at Sister, who ain't even half his size, then walks over to his cycle. "You calling this a motorbike? This machine ain't no motorbike. This here's a hawg."

"That's quite fitting," Sister says. "But we were talking about helmets. I know the results of not wearing one. I used to work in a hospital emergency room. It's too dangerous. You think you are taking this boy? No way."

She cranes her neck to look up at Jake, but she's not afraid of nothing. She could stuff a gorilla bigger than he is.

"Well, Toots, there ain't nothing you can do about it," Jake says, walking back to the Corvette and running his hand across the hood. "His daddy called me to come get him. I'm gonna do what he asks me to. And I'll make sure he don't fall off or nothing. Anyway, Matchstick's got a real hard head. Even if he does hit the ground, he won't break nothing important."

"Come here, Matchit," Babe says. She steps toward me and puts both arms around my shoulders, holding me tight in front of her.

"Get on the hawg, Matchstick." Jake lunges at me, nearly knocking Babe over, and grabs me by the arm.

"Get your hands off of him!" Sister says.

Jake don't like women trying to order him around. He picks me up by a belt loop and plunks me down on the motorcycle seat, then gets on in front of me. I see his arm reach to turn the key, and I feel him press his body back as he lifts his leg to draw back and stomp the crank. The smell of his greasy jacket makes me want to puke.

"You better put your arms around me, Barbie boy. You're gonna be taking a bite off the road if you don't." He laughs and jerks the wheel around. Two old women don't scare him.

I feel myself go weak, my heart's beating so fast it's about to pop out of me.

Babe's shaking all over. "Let me try to call Arnie again," she pleads. "I'm sure we can work things out." Poor Babe. She thinks talk fixes anything. She don't know Jake.

He roars the engine and adjusts his cowboy hat. "Sorry,

girls. No time for talk. Me and little Bubba here are heading out."

The motorcycle jerks forward. And Sister hollers, "Wait. You can have my car."

That stops Jake in his tracks. He's still on the bike, but he's got his boots on the ground.

"I'll make you a trade," Sister says. "My car for your motorbike. But you have to leave Matthew. That is, Matchit."

"You gotta be kidding." Jake clears his throat. "You're tricking me, ain't you?" He knows that car is worth a whole lot more than his old hawg.

Sister holds out her keys. She don't care what the car is worth. She wants that bike.

Jake is grinning like he just won the Daytona 500. He's practically drooling as he climbs off the motorcycle and walks to the passenger side of the Corvette, where Sister is standing with the door open. "The title is in the glove compartment," she says. He reaches across the smooth leather seats, opens the glove compartment, and pulls out a handful of papers. Sister signs the car title and shoves it back at Jake.

"Man," Jake keeps saying. He don't have enough different words in his brain to say how he feels. But he's happy, you can tell that. He climbs into the car, revs the engine, and backs out of the drive. All the way down the road, he's honking the horn and waving.

Ha! Matchstick, my brain says. Jake is your flesh and blood, but it didn't take him a second to give you away. He would've traded you for a chili cheese dog if he had the chance. You ain't nothing, boy.

No matter what my brain tells me, I know what just happened. Sister traded her mint-condition, hardly-ever-been driven, always-kept-in-the-garage, almost-never-even-been-rained-on '66 Corvette with knockoff wheels, side exhaust, the big block, and options—for Jake's old motorcycle. And for me.

Sister. She don't know nothing.

"Why in the world does your father leave you with that man?" Babe asks.

"He's a cousin," I tell her.

"Well, I don't care if he's the Pope's brother. From now on, you stay with us. And don't worry. I'll call your father and straighten out this whole misunderstanding."

Sister crosses her arms in front of her skinny self. I bet she don't weigh hardly nothing. One big wind could blow her all the way to Houston. Except for one thing. Her heart. It's pretty big, I figure.

"Want me to drive you home?" Babe asks her.

She shakes her head. "Take me over to Rice's Hardware. I have a new mode of transportation now. I need to see if they have any helmets."

"Want to go, Matchit?" Babe asks.

"Would you mind stopping at Lucky's?" I got something I got to pay for.

She don't ask no questions, just says that will be fine. I run out to my van before we leave. I know what I got to do.

"Still got those eagle eyes?" Sister asks a few minutes later when I've climbed into the backseat of the Mustang.

"Yes, ma'am." I want to say something about what she did. But I don't have the words.

"How's that pigeon doing?"

"Fine."

"Good," she says. "Guess I won't have to stuff him, will I?"

As we drive down the road toward Lucky's, she rolls down the window and sets her arm on the edge so that her elbow is sticking out. She must have been busy putting her hair into that knot thing on the back of her head when Babe called in a panic. One piece of hair is pinned up, the rest is falling down her back. I thought it was gray, but it's not. It's silvery brown and hangs curly down her back.

I can see her face in the rearview mirror. She's got her eyes closed.

"You okay?" Babe asks her.

"I'm happy as can be," she answers. "I got something I always wanted. A motorbike. Excuse me. A hawg."

That night Babe gets Daddy on the telephone. She tracks him down by calling the YMCA where he's been staying, and they forward her to the construction site after she insists it's an emergency. She tells him about Jake, how he didn't have helmets, and about how she wanted me to stay.

"Don't worry about it," she keeps telling him. I know he feels bad he got a kid who don't do nothing but cause trouble.

She hands the phone to me.

"Babe didn't steal nothing," I tell him.

"I know that," he says. "Why'd you make up all those lies?"

"I don't know," I mumble. All I can think about is I get scared inside. Being scared always makes me do things I don't want to.

"I'm sorry," I whisper, sniffing because I got a runny nose, because I might be getting a cold.

I chew on my lip, hoping everything gets all right.

"Come on, Match. You're going to have me crying, too."

"I ain't crying." I take a deep breath. Another deep breath.

"It's been nothing but one thing after another with the truck. I'm going to work here long enough to either buy something else or completely overhaul this thing."

"That could take forever."

"Nothing's forever, Match."

Chapter
TWENTY-FIVE

BABE CLAIMS THAT THE DAY I SET MY SUITCASE DOWN on her front steps the luck started up. She said it wasn't like a bolt of lightning. The luck came slow, making its way from the porch, down through the junkyard, and right up to the old school bus where Zebby lives. It wound its way through his arms and wrists all the way to his fingernails, and according to her, it ain't done yet. Before it's over, she says, Zebby will lie down with his face to the ground, press his hands onto the hot dry dirt, and feel the underground rivers moving to the sea. There will be enough luck for everybody.

Babe's got indigestion.

That's what I think.

For one thing, Zebby has had it. He's sick and tired of being an artist, sick and tired of his sculpture, which he can't seem to finish, no matter what he does.

From my bed I can see it, sticking up over the bus like a mast. I know. I been reading about that fisherman too much. I'm seeing boats everywhere. My brain's turning into a boat.

That sculpture ain't no sailboat, though. It ain't a warship, either. It ain't a rocket or a space station, or a missile. I already tried those ideas on it. Sometimes, the sun makes parts of it bright as fire. Parts are dark as caves and tunnels. At night, I've seen it turn into a black hole, then when I think it's gone for good, the moon turns its edges into silver. Sometimes I'm lying in bed watching it, trying to figure out what it is, and it shivers and moves in the darkness, then all the sudden it freezes into jagged steel. What is that thing? I've waited and waited on an answer. Zebby probably has, too. He can't wait no more.

It's morning when he walks up to the house. He's made a final decision. He's moving out of the junkyard, out of the bus, for sure and for good and forever. He's taken off his cap with the earflaps, taken off his leather apron and the leather gloves. He's got on new jeans and a shirt without holes, slip-on loafers instead of work boots. He's shaved his beard and cut his hair short, over the ears. He's got an I-give-up look on his face.

When I open the front door, he's standing there looking down at his feet. "Go get Babe," he tells me. "I'm moving out."

Babe's in the kitchen in her robe and slippers. I tell her about Zebby, and she picks up a box of Kleenex and heads to the front door. She's been expecting something like this, but it's still caught her off guard. She didn't want it to be this morning, this day.

"You're leaving? Now? Today?" she asks him.

"Soon. I've got to clean up things around the bus first."

"If it's about money, you can forget paying rent for a while. We can advertise some of your art. You'll start selling it again."

Zebby shakes his head. He don't want nobody paying his way.

"I'm finished," he says. "I've got to cut that mess apart, then you can sell the metal for scrap. I wanted you to know, in case you want to rent out the bus to another person who thinks he's a sculptor." He makes a slow sad grin at that joke.

"What are you going to do after you leave?"

"Maybe lay carpet," he says.

She shakes her head. "You're not a carpet layer." But he ain't convinced.

After he's gone, she explains it to herself and to me the best she knows how. Artists got temperaments. You're not supposed to understand them. Still, she is upset. Zebby's been around for a long time. It's not just that he's helped out with the yard, either. She says he's built beautiful things out of the old metal lying around the yard. It makes her feel like the junkyard is still alive. He belongs here, she says. She can't even imagine that he might leave. He will leave a hole in the yard too big to fill. She pulls out a handful of Kleenex.

It's the first time I've seen her sad.

I got to go outside. Got to try to stop him.

Zebby hasn't gone that far. I'm watching the backs of his shoes, listening to the soft shhhhh sound as they shuffle ahead of me in the dirt. I'm watching the way his body slumps forward, the way his head is bent down. The way his hands lie limp at his sides.

I move up beside him.

Walk with him through the dirt, through the weeds, around the cars.

I don't know what to say, but I got to say something.

"You can't quit," I tell him.

He keeps walking.

"You're just going to tear it up?"

"Yep," he says.

"You going to use a torch?"

"That's the idea."

Matchstick, that thing ain't nothing but pieces of a hundred wrecked cars melted together. I shake my head.

It's more than that. I saw it get welded in the night. Watched the sparks fly. Watched it grow until it took a bite out of the sky. Now it's going to be gone.

"Can't you wait a little longer? Maybe you'll figure it out."

Zebby walks faster. He don't want to hear about it no more.

I walk beside him, all the way to the bus door.

"Why can't you finish it?"

"Because it's futile," he says.

I don't know what futile means, but I know about quitting.

Zebby's eyes look like they died. There won't be nothing changing him.

"What do you think we should do?" I ask Dog that night. With my flashlight I see his eyes. Little yellow rings in the dark. He shuffles in his cage and I get out of bed and walk toward him. I slide my finger through the bars and stroke his soft feathers.

"You don't have nothing to say, do you?"

Dog don't have no answers, either.

I read a couple of pages of the fisherman book, but I can't get bored enough to fall asleep. And another thing. I feel sad. The old man's hands are still bleeding, and the boat has gotten lighter because most of the weight of the great fish is gone. It's true. The sharks get him.

My brain says You going to let a dumb book make you feel sad? It ain't even real.

Sorry. This book does seem real, even if it ain't.

Dog is watching me. His eyes are glowing. "You got an idea?" I whisper.

"Okay, boy. Let's go." The moon is still up and shining. Me and Dog. It'll be a great night for camping out.

Want to go through the tire tunnel? I ask Dog. He don't. It's a good thing. I got too much to carry. We take the long way, past the old Buick that's missing its wheels, past the Plymouth I got stuck in, past cars and pieces of cars, all the way to the van. When we get there, I set Dog on top. Then goes the blanket, pillow, and flashlight. Next, me. It's too nice of a night to sleep inside.

When we're settled, I shine the flashlight at the back of the house, where there's a row of sleeping pigeons under the eaves. "Do you see your friends?"

Dog rustles around in his cage, his cage which is too small for him, which was made for a parakeet. He can't even see that well through the bars. I feel sorry, sorrier than I feel for the old fisherman. Sorrier than I feel about Zebby. This bird ain't no parakeet. He don't belong in no parakeet cage.

"If I let you out," I whisper, "who knows what could happen? Freebie could show up again. You don't want that, do you?"

He don't know what he wants. He just sits there.

Sister says birds don't fly in the dark unless they get scared. I ain't planning on scaring him.

"When I turn this light off and let you out of your cage, you won't fly off. Right?" My whispers float on the darkness, reminding me of how quiet it is in the junkyard when Zebby's not welding or hammering.

I turn off the flashlight and gently open the door in the cage. "Come here, boy," I whisper to him, picking him up with both my hands. Slowly I pull him out.

Dog sits quiet with my hands cradled around him. "You're safe," I tell him. After a minute I spread my fingers apart just a little, then a little wider. I feel the sides of his body swell, his feathers push at my palms. Gradually, I open my hands all the way, wondering what he will do.

That bird don't even try to fly.

I set him down beside me on the van and hold my

breath. He shakes himself and tucks his head down. I figure he's happy camping out with me in the cool night air. We sit for a long time, both of us still as statues, and after a while I got my head on my knees. I'm sleepy, so sleepy I keep forgetting about staying awake, and over and over I almost shut my eyes. I tell myself a hundred times don't go to sleep. A thousand times. But my eyes don't pay attention.

The next thing I know, the moon is down and the sky is early-morning gray.

Dog? I whisper. I look around beside me on the roof of the van, on the hood, on the ground. He's gone.

I scramble to my feet and cup my hand over my eyes to see better. Squint at the telephone wires and poles, squint at the roof of the house, at the top of every wrecked car and truck in sight. My mouth is dry. My eyes sting, and my heart hurts. He's already made it out of the junkyard.

My brain starts to say how stupid I am for letting a bird sit beside me, how dumb I am for going to sleep. I hear all those things, but I ain't listening. Dog wanted to go. He chose it himself.

Still, I got a lump in my throat. "Dog?" I call. "You hiding?"

All around the yard, all the way out to Zebby's sculpture, I look again. Far to the edges of the field, out to the road toward town, to the edge of the world where the sun is coming up, then back to the sculpture, hoping a pigeon with a sewed-up throat might be sitting on top.

"Dog?" I call out into the morning darkness. "Dog?"

187

And then something else catches my attention.

It's the sculpture, its shape. The way it's bent, like a wishbone after you've made the wish and broke the bone, a curve slanting up into the sky. My eyes trace its form, its smooth gray edges, its gray body shooting into the morning, gray like river water, like the ocean, gray like something else, something big and real and alive.

What is it, Matchit?

"I know," I whisper. I finally know what that sculpture is.

Matchstick, you're crazy. First you camp out with a pigeon, then you take him out of his cage, then you let him fly away, and now this. You think you see a giant fish jumping into the sky. What's wrong with you, boy?

Ain't nothing wrong with me.

So why did Dog take off and leave you up here on top of this old van all by yourself? All the time you took care of him, read to him. You think you mattered to that pigeon?

What about that sculpture? Do you think it matters what you see? It's going to be torn up whether you care or not. Nothing matters, Matchstick McCarty.

Nothing.

I jump down from the van.

I've had enough camping out.

Chapter *Chapter* TWENTY-SIX

WHEN I TELL HER ABOUT DOG FLYING AWAY, Babe's not upset. She says it was time for him to go. "Besides," she says, "I feed those pigeons. He'll be back."

I doubt it.

Babe can't stand it. "You can't sit around moping," she says. She hands me a bucket of paint and a brush. "Go paint your van," she says.

I might as well.

It takes me all day and half the next.

My brain says You doing all this work for an old van that won't ever even see the road?

"Yep," I say. Besides, you never know.

Babe says it will sure brighten up the place to have a shiny red van in the middle of all that junk. She's right. When Daddy drives up, he won't have no trouble seeing it.

But just in case, I use my woodburning kit to make a sign: Matchit's Place.

After all my work is done, I'm outside at the edge of the house sitting on a stack of tires practicing my cast. On a real lake I bet I could cast inside a line of trees and never get tangled. I can hit my mark every time, which is now a coffee can instead of a box. I'm getting good, Babe says, nearly expert at casting. She says she might put a quarter on the ground. See if I can hit that.

I'm reaching my arm back, ready to cast again, when I see a green truck driving up the road. It's inching along, coming slow and quiet like a dog that's been yelled at for getting into the trash. As I cast my line in front of me, I watch the truck wind its way down the road all the way to the drive at the front.

It pulls to a stop.

I watch him get out. He's wearing the same black Wranglers and the same shirt he had on when he left. You can tell he hasn't shaved in a couple of days. Probably hasn't even combed his hair. He stretches and takes off his cap. Nope. He hasn't combed his hair. He looks tired.

"Match," he says, walking up to me. He tries to say something else, but his voice cracks.

I want to ask where's Jewel, but I hold my tongue. It's plain she didn't come back.

"Match, I'm sorry I'm so late."

I'm about to say something smart, but his eyes don't let me. I jump down from the tires. I set my rod and reel down in the dirt, and he hugs me, and when he starts to cry, I hug him back. I ain't never seen my daddy cry.

He tells me that Jewel wanted to come with him, but she needed two or three more days to get her things together, do a little more shopping, get her nails done, and say good-bye to her friends. And the last thing. She wanted to be taken home before he stopped to get me. That did it. He says he can't believe he could've been so blind.

Maybe you were just scared, I tell him.

He looks at me long and hard.

Packing ain't that bad. Folding up my clothes is easy. I don't got much. Mostly what I came with, except for my birthday shirt from Mama and a couple of extra jeans and T-shirts from Babe. I got my lucky eagle eyes and my four-leaf clover key chain, the manual for the van, and a few other things. It all goes in my suitcase. I got my drawing supplies, my woodburning kit, a bulldog hood ornament from a Mack truck that Babe gave me. Finally, I got my box of license plates. And my bike. Everything is ready to go.

"Wait," Babe says, "I called Sister. She's on her way. Matchit McCarty, you aren't leaving until you say good-bye to everyone."

"Want me to put your bike in the back of the truck?" Daddy asks.

I say yes, and he loads it up along with my suitcase and the box of license plates, each plate wrapped in paper so nothing will get scratched.

In a few minutes Sister comes riding up on Jake's motorcycle. When Daddy sees her, he says, "Man, that bike looks just like my cousin's." Me and Babe look at each other. We don't say nothing.

Sister climbs off the bike and marches straight toward me. "What's this about you leaving? You haven't learned how to do taxidermy yet. You haven't run any errands for me on that bicycle. You think you can take off just when the work starts?"

"I guess," I say. She don't mean nothing.

"You want to walk over to Zebby's and tell him goodbye, Matchit?" Babe asks.

I shake my head. Zebby don't like to be bothered. Besides, he's got his own packing to do.

Before we leave, Babe makes us promise that we'll come back for her New Year's celebration. I tell her we'll come. I promise.

"And Arnie, if you have to work out of town, leave Matchit here, okay?" she asks.

Daddy says he will. But he's planning on finding some local jobs.

I ain't holding my breath on that one.

Babe hugs Daddy, then she turns to me. I don't stiffen up or nothing. She got to do about ten hugs, cry and talk the whole time.

Sister ain't the hugging type. She got her arms crossed at her waist. She got a frown on her face. My brain says You better leave her alone. She might bite.

My arms could just about go around her twice, she's so

skinny. Shoot, she's got bones like a bird's. They'd snap if you hugged too hard.

"Good-bye," I tell her.

"Good-bye," she says back.

The new truck seats are smooth. No duct tape, no cigarette burns. A hundred and thirty thousand miles on the odometer ain't too bad. Plus it's got a new timing chain, new belts. "She's running like a baby," Daddy brags.

Sister and Babe stand at the drive while we back out, Babe waving, Sister holding herself tight. And I take one last look at the sculpture, Zebby's fish.

"It's been a long summer," Daddy says when we get on the road.

I look back through the rear window. I wonder how long it will take Zebby to cut apart his sculpture piece by piece with his torch. I wonder if the pieces will fall to the ground one by one, or if the whole thing will topple over. Will he stack the broken parts into a pile, then load them up and haul them away?

"How's the bike doing?" Daddy asks, interrupting my thoughts.

"Fine," I answer, feeling a little sad. Is it because I got a new silver bicycle that I can't even ride or is it because I'm seeing Zebby's art broken to pieces? I stare into the truck bed, watching my suitcase slide to the tailgate, watching my box of license plates bounce with the potholes in the road.

"Everything okay back there in the bed?" Daddy asks.

I say yes, and he swerves just enough for the box of

license plates to slide across the back. Over three hundred plates. If each one was worth only a dollar, I'd have over three hundred dollars. They're worth a lot more than that, though. It could be a bundle of cash. Cash I could spend in a lot of ways. Cash you could live on if you had to. And then I think of Zebby.

I swing my body around, facing the front. "I got to go back," I say. "Please. I got to."

Daddy looks over at me, his eyes red with tiredness.

"It's really important. I mean, really important." I don't explain that those license plates just told me what to do. Told me how to help Zebby wait on laying carpet. Daddy might not understand.

He yawns and looks over at me. I figure he's about to say no that he's too tired, but he don't. He just yawns again and slows to a stop on the side of the road. He backs up the truck and turns around. "I'm not in any hurry. Not this time," he says.

When we pull into the front drive, Babe and Sister are gone. That's okay. This is something I got to do by myself.

"Need some help?" Daddy asks.

Nope.

He leans back and pulls his cap over his eyes. "I'll take a snooze. I'm beat, almost no sleep in the last couple of days. You go on. Do what you need to do."

I jump out of the truck and walk around to the bed.

I lift the box of license plates out of the truck, thinking about what I'm going to do. I got an excited feeling about how much money these things might bring, probably as much as you'd make laying carpet in a bunch of houses.

I carry the box between the cars, through the tall grass and weeds, past my van, all the way through the junkyard, all the way to Zebby's bus.

Parts of the sculpture are lying on the ground, pieces of jagged metal that have been cut apart. Zebby's tools are lying next to them. I don't take time to see how much of the sculpture is gone, I just set down the box and pound on the bus.

I can see him inside, sitting at his table, drawing. He sets his pencil down and looks up. When he sees it's me, he walks to the door and turns the inside crank to open it, then he pokes his head out.

"I'm leaving," I tell him.

"Oh," he says.

"My father came." I look down at my feet. I got over three hundred license plates in this box, all colors, all clean and shiny. I got the whole United States of America and more, right here and ready to sell.

I pick up the box and hand it to him. "Here."

"It's heavy," he says. "What is it?"

"Just a present. From me." And then I add, "For you to sell, if you want to. So you won't have to lay carpet." He wrinkles his forehead. He don't get it.

I turn to walk away. I take one more look at the sculpture.

"I'm gonna miss that fish."

"Fish?" Zebby says.

195

I take a deep breath and point. "Look at it."

He steps outside and looks up.

He don't see nothing.

"You got to squint."

His eyes got a blank look.

"See how it's gray? How it's jumping?" My heart beats faster. That thing's just about got water splashing up around it.

Zebby's squinting real good now. He's looking, really looking, tracing the sculpture with his eyes like he ain't never seen it before.

"You still going to tear it up?"

Zebby don't answer. He's got a faraway look in his eyes. Maybe he's thinking he don't want to lay carpet no more.

And then it's time to go.

Good-bye. Short and simple.

When I get back to the truck, Daddy's snoring. You wake him up, you're waking up one bad mood. I ain't chancing it, even if there ain't nothing to do.

Except for one thing. The bicycle.

"Okay, Matchit McCarty," I say to myself. "It's time."

My heart is scared, but it feels good, too. It knows what it has to do.

I lift out my bike. Set it on the ground. You think I'm afraid I might break my neck? Break my arm? Split my lip? That ain't it at all. I ain't afraid of none of that stuff. But I am afraid, just a little.

I roll the bike down the road, away from the house and

the truck. I know how to get on. That's the easy part. One foot on the pedal, one to push off on the ground.

I can't keep count of how many times I fall. It's too many. I got holes in both knees of my jeans, but I pick myself up every time and start over, and ride a few feet, then a couple of yards, a couple of feet, then finally I'm wobbling down the road away from the junkyard.

The sun is looking down at me. It's saying you done a good thing, Matchit McCarty. The wind is swirling all around me, patting me on the back, blowing my hair, showing me how good it feels to ride a bike.

Matchit, you go, boy! I ride ride ride, like I done it my whole life.

When I get back to the truck, Daddy opens his eyes and stretches. "So what've you been doing?"

Nothing much, I tell him.

"Ready?" he asks.

"Yep," I say. I'm ready.

ABOUT THE AUTHOR

MARTHA MOORE lives in Mansfield, Texas. When she was a child, she looked out the kitchen window one morning and saw twenty-seven old boats stacked all over the backyard. In this wonderful playground, she invented many stories and poems. When she grew up, she became a teacher and writer. She believes every child is gifted. And she loves junkyards.